Speed-Walk and Other Stories

Drue Heinz Literature Prize 2003

Speed-Walk

and Other Stories

Suzanne Greenberg

To Barbara,
Once a Literary Woman,
always a Literary Woman!
Best,
Suanne Cohen
1/04

University of Pittsburgh Press

Published by the University of Pittsburgh Press, Pittsburgh, Pa., 15260

Copyright © 2003, Suzanne Greenberg

All rights reserved

Manufactured in the United States of America

Printed on acid-free paper

10 9 8 7 6 5 4 3 2 1

ISBN 0-8229-4217-8

To Michael, for remembering what matters

Contents

Speed-Walk   1

The Yes Button   9

The Queen of Laundry   20

Two Parties   29

Fumes   34

Indoor-Outdoor Pool   49

Repeat After Me   59

Cheap Clown   89

A Good Bet   95

You Can't Dance   101

My Treat, Geronimo   108

Aghast   117

Mr. Herzinger   122

Naked Lake   128

Honeymoon   135

The Visit   142

Biloxi   161

Perm   165

Acknowledgments   171

Speed-Walk and Other Stories

Speed-Walk

Two months after my wife, Becky, died, I went on my first speed-walking date. I followed behind Corrine and watched her thighs move. Tight and brown, they reminded me of roasted chicken legs. They made me hungry for a kind of take-out Becky used to bring home. I didn't know where to find it. I pumped my arms as I walked, the way I'd seen others do, so it looked, I hoped, as if I were hard at work.

When we got back to Corrine's house, her daughter-in-law was bench-pressing her baby on the couch in the living room, both of them wearing bright orange T-shirts, the television on mute. We walked by them on our way to the patio, and for a moment the baby's fat diaper, with its comforting powder smell, passed in front of my face.

I followed Corrine through her shining kitchen out back to the hot tub. She sat on the wooden ledge and kicked her feet to an efficient, private beat. Everything exercise.

Still wearing my gym shorts, I lowered my body in and tried to convince myself that this was different than taking an actual bath together. I positioned myself so a jet was poised against my lower back. This felt not altogether pleasant, as if I were having a single, neglected tooth cleaned. Before Becky died, I never understood people who claimed they had simply ended up somewhere or with someone or in some job, but now maybe I was starting to.

"You can bet they're not doing this in Chicago right now," Corrine said to me.

As I walked up the street toward my house, slowed down as I always was by the lump of hill, I could hear my seeing-eye dog barking in the living room. Twice a day, I had to clean the saliva off the window he barked onto. He jumped on me when I walked in, followed me until I shut the bathroom door against him, and whined as I showered off warm chlorine.

The dog was Becky's retirement project, but she died before she'd finished training him. Becky had always had an idea or two going, and without her around, I didn't seem to have any. In Chicago, she had taken a single class and come home and sponge-painted our entire kitchen purple. Our backyard was full of compost and tomato plants, and our thirty-eight-year-old daughter's first drawings were laminated and arranged on the wall of the den.

In California, she had just gotten started. Training the dog was it. The Guide Dog of America people had warned against getting too attached. "Let's just call him the dog for now," she'd said, rubbing him behind his ears. All our friends in Chicago had grandchildren, but our daughter wasn't even on her first marriage. Before Becky's urine had turned bright red, she'd set off with the dog down the street several times a day, his leash twisted short and tight around her hand.

After Becky died, the guide dog people decided they didn't want him back. At the volunteer luncheon in Sylmar, a Guide Dog of America official tapped me on the shoulder when I was in the middle of eating my peach cobbler, took me into the small blank room, in which moments earlier Becky's dog had been evaluated, and told me that the dog was ruined, and for a hundred dollars he was mine. The dog smiled up at me and offered his paw, the one trick I had taught him myself to amuse Becky. "Cute," the official said, "but completely useless."

*

When the doorbell rang, I turned down the Simon and Garfunkel record that I had taken to listening to during the day while I folded my laundry, rinsed out the coffeepot, and generally padded around my little house as if I were trespassing. The music depressed and stirred me. I felt buoyant with suffering, part of a huge arc of human failure.

Corrine's daughter-in-law and her baby stood at my front door, their thin blond hair in high ponytails above their ears, their rounded bellies exposed between black gym shorts and yellow shirts that looked as if they had been peeled open in front like bananas. "Christ, I hate to bother you like this," the daughter-in-law said.

"I didn't know she could walk yet."

"Well, I am sort of helping her up a little," the daughter-in-law said, and I could see now how the baby's head was propped against her mother's knee.

"A-hoo," the baby said to me.

"She doesn't really talk yet either," the daughter-in-law said. "Hell, she's only thirteen months. What do people expect?"

I tried to remember what to expect at thirteen months. My own daughter was nearly middle-aged now. It was her Simon and Garfunkel record.

"She looks fine to me," I said.

"A-hoo," the baby said and pointed next to my leg. I looked down at the dog who put out his paw. The baby reached forward to take it and fell into my house.

"What am I thinking? Come in," I said. The baby crawled over to the couch, where she pulled herself up and gurgled at the dog who stayed by her side.

"Maybe he thinks the baby is another dog. He's not that quick," I said.

"Here's what I was wondering," Corrine's daughter-in-law said, still close enough to the entranceway to be neither completely in nor outside my house. "What would you think about giving us a ride to the mall?" I looked around for an excuse, but everything looked in order.

"Can you give me five minutes?"

*

On the seat next to me in the car, the baby bounced around on Corrine's daughter-in-law's lap. I remembered my own daughter loose in the backseat, hopping from one window to the other, depending on the view, but weren't there laws now, complicated provisions about car seats and seat belts?

"Is she okay like that?" I said. The daughter-in-law waved her hand at me in a gesture of dismissal.

"What are we talking about here? Two, three miles?" She pulled down the visor and, while her baby bounced, examined her teeth in a mirror I didn't even know was there. Becky had always applied her makeup before we left the house and then left it alone.

Becky's seeing-eye dog sighed heavily in the backseat, as if commenting on the general dullness of things. The baby wouldn't stop crying until I agreed to take the dog along with us, and now I was stuck with him for the foreseeable future.

"We're Baby Spice," Corrine's daughter-in-law said to me, "in case you were wondering. You don't think it's a problem that the group broke up, do you?"

"Certainly not," I said, although I had no idea what she was talking about. I longed for nothing more than to be back in my quiet little house.

"A-hoo," the baby said to me.

"But you can call me Rose. Not Rosy, whatever you do. Man, I hate that."

The parking lot at the mall was crowded, despite the fact that it was Saturday and seventy degrees and sunny. Back in Chicago, if we had weather like this in the middle of February, everyone would be standing outside looking startled, as if jet planes had just landed on each of our front lawns.

"There's just the matter of the entrance fee now," Rose said to me as we walked through the lot, the baby squirming in her arms to touch the dog that I walked between us. I had the dog in full training harness, the way I always did when I had to take him somewhere dogs weren't normally allowed. I found there was no need to wear dark sunglasses. I'd simply give into a dazed fog I'd been fighting off since Becky's death, and no one ever asked me any questions. "But you can bet we'll be winning it back for you momentarily. You don't know what it means to me, a near-total stranger like you believing in me this way when him and his whole family don't."

Once, two weeks after Becky died, I came to this mall at eight A.M. on a Tuesday for free coffee and donuts and to circle the perimeter before the stores opened with fellow senior citizens. Senior Day. The donuts were small and dirt brown, and everyone seemed already to belong to informal groups, and I didn't come back. Instead I began to wander my own new neighborhood, which is how I met Corrine, and which is how, I supposed, I was led into this very situation.

It turned out the entrance fee for the Mother-Daughter Look-Alike Contest Rose planned to enter was only twenty dollars, so I paid it, pretending to finger the money in my wallet as if finger-reading the denominations.

"Cool, Gramps," a teenage boy said to me. He handed Rose two white squares of cardboard with the number 68 printed on them in red. I helped her peel off the adhesive and centered one of the squares on her back.

"Mommy's putting wings on you, sweetie," Rose told the baby, who held onto my knee. "Stay still just a minute."

All around us were mothers and daughters, wearing matching numbers, straightening out each other's makeup and examining each other's teeth for pieces of food. Despite their matching hairdos and outfits, Rose's baby looked more like the other babies than she did her mother. I picked out the mother-daughter set I thought would win: an adolescent girl and a woman in her late thirties who wore big skirts and red neckties and had the same wounded-looking, eager faces. Rose pulled the baby away from my leg and held her up in the air.

"We'll show that daddy and grandma of yours what's what," she said. Becky's dog pulled at his harness, and I told Rose I was going to take him for a walk and come back soon. I let him lead me away from the Mother-Daughter contest to the food court, where the smells were large and urgent and where the dog tugged harder. He sniffed at a garbage can, and a woman held her burrito away from her mouth and pointed at him to her friend.

"I thought they weren't supposed to do that," she said.

"Shh," her friend said. "Just because he's blind doesn't mean he can't hear."

"What did I say that was so terrible?" the other woman said, clamping down on her food.

Maybe they were sisters, not friends, I thought. I pulled the dog away from the garbage can and slowly circled the edge of the food court until I found a smell that was so familiar I nearly sat down on the floor and wept. Instead I stood in line and waited for my turn. Behind me in line, someone whispered, "Their other senses are highly developed."

"I'll take a bucket of legs," I said when my turn came. I paid my money, stepped to the right, and was handed a white beach bucket full of roasted chicken legs. I found a spot at the end of a long table and sat down. The dog reached out his paw to me. I put a leg on the ground, and only after the dog had snatched it did I remember Becky's warnings about bone splinters. I had forgotten to order a drink, and it seemed too late for that now, so I ate just two legs and put the bones back in the bucket. I thought about Becky bringing home this chicken for me and how I was now going to bring it home for myself and how this wasn't the same thing at all.

I pulled the dog back out toward the area of the mall where the contest was being held. A tight circle had formed around the mother-daughters, but people moved apart to let us in. Two women with curly red hair and lots of gold-colored jewelry stepped into the center of the circle when their number was called out. They spun around in front of the judges in unison, then shook their wrists in the air as if their bracelets were tambourines. The crowd applauded and the dog barked. All around the inside of the circle were mother-daughter look-alikes, smiling hard at the judges who sat behind a long card table. I looked around for Rose and the baby but didn't see them. Then someone pulled at my hair. I turned around, and the baby said, "A-hoo." Rose said, "Ready to roll?"

Rose didn't talk as we walked through the parking lot, the baby tight against her body, and I thought about several different ways of asking her what had happened but thought better of each one of them. I put the bucket of chicken legs down on the seat between us and didn't say anything when, the baby on her lap, Rose dug in.

"Fine print, my ass," she finally said. "Who ever heard of disqualifying someone because they couldn't turn around on their own in front of the judges yet? At least they should have given me my money back."

My money, I thought, but I didn't say anything.

"Slow down here for a minute, would you?" Rose said.

I couldn't imagine driving any slower than I already was, as worried as I was about the baby loose on her mother's lap in the front seat, so I pulled over by the side of the road in front of a strawberry stand.

"Hey, Rosy! Is that you?" the man behind the stand called out.

"I said 'slow down,' not 'stop,'" Rose said, but she was already putting the baby down and pushing the car door open with her pink sneaker.

I put the baby on my lap and let her pretend to drive while her mother leaned over the rows of strawberries and talked. She got back into the car and slipped a piece of paper into her pocketbook. "High school," she said. "At least I didn't marry *him.*"

When we pulled up to the front of their house, Corrine was watering the front yard in her bathing suit. She started to wave at us and then stopped and frowned and turned the water off. I threw a leg in the back for the dog, dumped the rest out on the street, and handed the baby the bucket. "For the beach," I said.

"A-hoo," the baby said, reaching for the bucket's handle and grabbing the air next to it instead.

"I mean, she just turned one," Rose said to me, taking the bucket. "What do people expect?"

I watched them walk to the front door and then drove my car down the hill and around the block, the long way to my house. I pulled into my driveway and shut off the engine. The dog sighed heavily in the backseat, his chicken leg devoured. Tomorrow morning, I'd bring the DustBuster out to the car and clean up bone chips that he missed, but for now I stared at my little house, this place where, after so much time, I had ended up living.

The Yes Button

When Carson's daughters take him to lunch, he sits between them at the sushi bar and feels as if he's flanked by prostitutes. They're too old for him to tell them how to dress and even if they weren't, what would he say? What wouldn't make him look like a fool or a dirty old man? The sushi bar is surrounded by floor-to-ceiling windows. Above the bar is a huge open skylight. As has been the case for the three days that he's been in California, he's at a loss to say whether he's truly indoors or out.

His oldest daughter, Summer, takes a surprisingly old-fashioned pair of tiny, rectangular reading glasses out of her purse and squints at the bill when it comes. She has complicated hair, long where it should be short and short where it should be long. It falls in her face and Carson resists the temptation to stick it behind her ear. "All righty, then," she finally says, laying out the money. His daughters talk in ways that sound as if they might be ironic but actually aren't. This is their treat, they've insisted. The one restaurant he didn't pick himself, the one meal he's not paying for.

He follows behind his daughters to his rental car, which is parked behind the restaurant. They both wear short shorts, tank tops and fuzzy brown ankle boots, the boots a small concession to November, he supposes. Carson's younger daughter, Willow, is taking flamenco dancing lessons at her community college and walks with her arms floating in the air, and he worries that at any minute she might decide to stomp her feet and break into all-out dance. He watched a flamenco dancer once when he was on a failed date at a Spanish restaurant. Both the date and the restaurant now feel vague to him but somehow the flamenco dancer doesn't. With her pouty mouth and loud feet, she seemed to Carson like a four-year-old having a tantrum.

Now, Carson catches a glimpse of what appears to be an inky tattoo on Willow's lower back as her tank top rides up with her arms, and he quickly looks away. Already over the past several days he has seen a stud flash on Summer's tongue, a toe-ring on he can't remember which one of his daughters.

His girls sit behind him in the car, and one of them shouts out, "Get a move on, driver," and the other one giggles. They are twenty and twenty-three. Although he's paid his child support on time each month since the divorce—not even allowing for a grace period of a few days, the way he does with the electric bills and, on occasion, the mortgage—Carson hasn't seen either of his daughters in eight years, and he can't begin to tell their voices apart without looking back.

When he pulls up to their mother's condominium, Carson considers getting out and walking them in but thinks better of it. He's wearing sunglasses but it's late afternoon and the sky itself, a drenched blue, seems to be bothering his eyes. The girls' mother lives in one of those places that gives nothing away from its flat outside gate and stucco walls, but he knows what's inside and feels way too tired today to steel himself against the aggressively lush landscaping, the waterfalls and walking bridges, the eerie indoor mall feeling that leaves him stoned and slow-witted and that southern California developers have somehow managed to replicate outside in these kind of places.

Back home, people don't live this way. They have backyards that need to be mowed. Sometimes they have dogs. He himself has a dog in his backyard at home right now. Carson wonders if he actually remembered to ask the paperboy to watch the dog or just planned to, if he left out enough food and water or if squirrels ate the food and Max, his dog, knocked over his water and even now is resorting to sucking the soil for moisture.

He hadn't intended to worry about his dog while he was gone. In fact, he hadn't quite intended to be gone. So often had he planned this trip in his head and then failed to follow through in the outside world that requires complicated planning, reservations, plane tickets and leave from work and rides to the airport, that he hadn't quite realized he was actually leaving until the plane took off and the pilot told them their flight should be a smooth one and to sit back and relax for the next five hours. He rarely ever went anywhere for more than a day, and now here he was in California with his two grown daughters getting out of the backseat of his rental car and blowing him kisses goodbye.

*

Something goes wrong for Carson after he drops off his girls and gets back to his hotel. His magnetic key doesn't light up long enough for him to let himself in. He tries it five times in a row, each time feeling more and more as if he's breaking in or watching his credit card get rejected. Although he's alone in the hallway, Carson feels as if he's holding up a long line of people anxious for him to get a move on. *Deadbeat*, they whisper, *lowlife*.

Instead of asking at the front desk for a new key, he goes to the bar and orders scotch neat. The hotel bar is a reassuringly dark and uncomplicated place. It is clearly inside. When Carson reaches in his coat pocket for his wallet, he feels the cell phone one of his girls gave him to use while he's here in case he gets lost on the freeway. Who would he call, he wondered. Them? Was he already so old he had to rely upon his daughters for such basic needs as directions? Easier to stay nearby and take the surface streets than contemplate this question.

Carson phones his ex-wife with his daughter's telephone. He's relieved, when she answers, that it's not one of his daughters. She's never required the kind of small talk he feels obligated to keep up with them. "I'm drunk and I need someone to drive me home," he says.

"Okay, where are you?" Deena says. He can hear her breath quicken. She's already applying her lipstick; she's already searching for her car keys; she's already on her way to save him. There are moments like this when he wonders why he didn't try harder to convince her to stay and work it out.

"Hotel bar," he says.

"Can you give me a little more to go on? Name, location, anything?"

"My hotel bar, Deena. I just wanted to talk to you."

"Damn you," she says, but he hears her smacking her lips together to even out her lipstick.

*

By the time she gets to the bar, he is, in fact, a little drunk. He knows this not because his ex-wife looks to him like some kind of wispy gypsy mirage of someone's fantasy of a sexy backup singer— she really does look this way—but because when he stands up to greet her, he can't remember what's expected of him, a handshake, a cheek kiss, or, even possibly some type of hug. She dissipates his confusion by simply sitting down across from him at the little round table he's chosen and rolling back her shoulders just enough to release her shawl.

"Community college," Carson says. "Why not four-year state schools at least? That's the kind of thing I wanted to talk about."

Deena orders a seltzer with lemon and then glares at him. "It's a little late to get involved with their education, isn't it?" she says. "Besides, that's the way they do things out here. They'll transfer in their units later."

He doubts either one will be transferring in anything but decides to drop it. In truth, his daughters don't seem all that bright to him. He imagines them studying their fingernails in class, deciding whether or not to try a new color later that afternoon, while some weary, over-worked community college professor drones on.

"I almost forgot. You've got a message from someone who claims to be your paperboy," Deena says. She opens up her purse, pulls out a piece of paper folded neatly down the middle and hands it to him. "He says he doesn't think it's urgent but to call before ten tonight anyways." *Anyways*. He sits with this word for a minute. Not that he's exactly lived up to any huge potential himself with his mediocre state government "career"—he can't help but think of the word career in relation to himself in anything but quote marks. Even now he imagines he might do something else, something dynamic and life-altering with young people, or at least the word *youth* might be in his title, as in Director of Youth Programs or Youth Coordinator. But, really, how could he have married a woman who said anyways? Of course they divorced. How else could things have turned out? Still, sitting across from his ex-wife, slightly drunk now in the hotel bar, he remembers other bits and pieces that were once part of them, a nightgown she wore when she nursed the girls, the slits her breasts fit through.

"We've all been wondering," she says, "you know, what's the matter with you."

"The matter?" he says. He shakes the image of the nightgown out of his mind and sorts through his ailments. A recurring fungus caught between the two smallest toes on his left foot, a molar that has recently become sensitive to cold. Lately, too, there's the vague sense of mis-directed urgency, almost a panic really, that his body seems to absorb from the air itself each day in the mid-afternoon. But she wouldn't be asking about any of that.

"It's okay," she says, "if you don't want to talk about it." She's wearing her best thoughtful look. Deena reaches across the table as if she is about take his hand and pat it but instead places a finger on a quarter left on the table and pushes it around in a small circle. "I mean, why else would you be out here after so much time? The girls and I figured it out. Together."

Then he gets it. Cancer. Heart disease. Lymphoma.

"Oh, right," he says. His real reasons for finally coming out to see them—guilt, curiosity, boredom with his own life—seem suddenly embarrassingly trivial.

"I guess it's bedtime, then," she says. And for a moment he thinks she may actually follow him into the elevator and up to his room, and he worries about the faulty door card, that something so small could ruin such a moment.

But when he stands up and walks with her to the door of the bar, she says goodbye there. He watches her guide her body across the lobby, her shoulders held in that small, calm way that still makes men look up from their drinks and newspapers.

*

After checking his driver's license, the woman at the front desk takes his card away, runs it through a small machine and hands it back to him without an apology. He opens the door to his room just in time to hear the phone.

"He's not happy," the voice at the other end of the line tells him. "What makes you think he can even appreciate the shape of his food? Do you think dogs actually know if their food is shaped like bones? Why not television-shaped dog food?"

"Do I know who this is?" he says.

"Why not tiny penises for that matter?"

"Should I know you?"

"Were you even going to return my call? Don't tell me the ex didn't pass on the message. Don't try to play that one."

"I get it. You're the paperboy. What's wrong? Is Max sick?"

"Do you even care? Because I'm thinking if you cared you might add a can or two here and there. You might add, shall we say, just a smidge more variety to his diet."

"Fine," he says. He tries to remember who this lunatic of a paperboy is, what he offered to pay him. "Buy what you want. I'll reimburse you when I get back on Thursday."

"I'm thinking lamb chunks maybe, none of that pureed horsemeat shit."

"Fine," Carson says.

"Nothing big, dammit. Just a can or two here or there for variety's sake."

*

The next day Carson sleeps late and spends the morning in bed reading the real estate section and marveling at how little he could afford to buy if he were planning to move across the country. When his daughters call with their plan to take him to Universal Studios, he remembers his alleged illness and tells them he needs a day off, a break, is what he says. He'll see them tonight instead when they pick him up for the concert.

That night, he sits in the front next to Deena, his two daughters in the back. The car smells of moist women, their conditioners and face creams and breath mints and lip glosses. It's as if they're all out on some kind of lucky collective date. Carson thinks about property, how if he were to somehow pull his family back together at this late date, the four-bedroom house in Massachusetts that he once shared with a girlfriend but now shares with no one but his dog would equal a two-bedroom townhouse in California that he could share with his wife and two daughters.

Then, as if to interrupt his calculations, Deena pulls over suddenly in front of an apartment building, and a man walks up toward the car. "My boyfriend, Henry," she says. "Be nice."

Carson knows part of what *be nice* means is that he should get out and offer the surprise boyfriend the front seat. But he thinks, fuck it, and lets Henry slide on in the back. He had hoped to get more pleasure out of watching him do this, but Henry somehow makes it look not only painless to squeeze himself into such a small space, but desirable. He smiles and stretches his arm out around Carson's daughters as if he's got the best seat in the house. "It's so cool you're here, guy," the boyfriend says. "So cool you're doing this."

Carson feels his neck strain and turns back around to face front.

"Being the family man and everything after so much time, I mean," Henry says from the back.

The concert is in a park. They step around blankets full of rosy blond children and cheese plates and bottles of wine until they find a spot that Henry deems okay. He parks them all in front of a group of tightly toned women spread out on a blanket, feeding each other broccoli florets with dip. "Lesbos," Henry whispers, elbowing him in the side.

The Municipal Band plays enthusiastically yet badly, but no one seems to notice. Henry dances with Carson's wife and each of his daughters while Carson sits in the lawn chair they've brought for him, as if he's the lame uncle or perhaps the grandfather taken out for the day from the nursing home. The lesbians on the blanket behind him are taking turns demonstrating what appear to be elaborate yoga postures. He can see them out of the corner of his eye, their tanned thighs and sinewy forearms, but he feels as if he's staring straight at them and tries to face more fully forward. He's never thought much about lesbians before, wouldn't have even realized these women were lesbians if Henry hadn't told him, but now he can't stop thinking about them. Lesbians, lesbians, lesbians.

When his cell phone rings, he doesn't recognize the sound; thinks perhaps it's coming from the band, maybe some attempt at catching up with the times, until one of the lesbians behind him taps him on the shoulder and says, "You're ringing, guy."

Carson takes a moment to register what she means and then finds the phone in his pocket, stares at it until he finds the "Yes" button to press.

"I'm thinking maybe you don't even deserve this dog. That's what I'm thinking," the voice on the other end says.

"Oh, Jesus," Carson says. "You again."

"Do you think you can just put an animal on autopilot? When I called the vet to check on his rabies vaccine after the biting incident, do you know what they told me? All his boosters are expired. You're lucky about the rabies. Just under the wire on that one. Do you know how sick a dog could get? Do you even know what could happen?"

"Biting incident?" Carson asks, but the phone line is dead now. Either the paperboy has hung up on him or one of those mysterious cell phone things has happened and he's simply been cut off. Before he has a chance to search his pockets futilely for the note from his ex-wife with the paperboy's number and try to call back and tell him that Max does not bite, has never bitten anyone in his entire life, his daughters are pulling him up to dance to a rendition of "Brown Sugar" so giddy and sanitized that he first mistakes it for Rogers and Hammerstein.

All the rosy blond children are being pulled to their feet by their parents. The lesbians are up now and dancing, too. Henry moves over their way, tries a little hip movement in their direction. Carson feels dizzy with confusion as his daughters—the flamenco lesson one doing something fluttery with her arms—and ex-wife shimmy in front of him with their remotely familiar bodies and faces.

*

When he walks into the lobby of his hotel two hours later, a voice calls him over to the check-in area. "Messages," the woman behind the desk says, and hands him a small stack of papers. "I remember you. You're the one who had the door card problem. First that, now this."

Her face is scrubbed clean, no make-up except for thick, dark lipstick that, when she speaks, seems to keep moving a microsecond longer than her lips actually move. Lesbian? Carson wonders.

"I've asked the manager, and we don't have a fast and firm policy on this, but we may just have to cut you off if these don't level off soon."

Carson cannot stop watching her mouth. It's as if she's being dubbed. He finally turns and walks toward the elevator, hoping his room card won't cause him any more trouble. "I mean it's not as if we don't try to be accommodating, but it's not as if you're our only guest here either," she shouts.

In his room, Carson sits at the little ornamental desk and reads the messages one at a time. Then he spreads them out around the second bed, the one that he doesn't sleep in, notes the time scribbled on top of each, and tries to place them in order. Apparently it comes down to this: Max is in hiding. He can only be walked at night since the biting incident. *In complete darkness*, one of the notes says. He is in hiding *for his own good. GOOD NEWS!* Another note reads. *The said victim has been spotted limping around the neighborhood in her soccer uniform—how many stitches could it have been anyway, we have to wonder????*

*

In the morning, Carson phones his wife to tell her that he's leaving earlier than he planned, and Henry answers the phone. "Hey, there!" Henry says in place of hello.

"So, you sleep over there," Carson says. "With my daughters in the house, you sleep over?"

"Whoa there, guy," Henry says. "Good thing Deena warned me about your east coast sarcasm."

When Carson tells her that he's changed his ticket, Deena insists on driving him to the airport. He waits for her in front of the hotel, plans to tell her in the car that they were wrong about him, that he's really fine. It's just that some sick fuck of a paperboy is up to something with his dog, a dog he's just now realized he cares about more than he'd like to admit. But she's not alone. They're all in the backseat, his daughters and Henry, each smiling sympathetically up at him.

On the way to the airport they get stuck in traffic, and his daughters insist they play a car game. "I'm going to my aunt's house!" one of them shouts, and they each say what they plan to pack in their suitcases. When it's Carson's second turn, he screws up, passes over Henry's dumbbells, calls Summer's purple iris a pink carnation.

"Out, out, out," Deena tells him. She puts her hand on his knee and pats it as if to console him. He wonders if Henry sees this from the backseat. Deena moves her hand from his knee to the radio controls, puts on a station that gives the traffic report "on the sixes."

Deena switches freeways and suddenly has them in the carpool lane, is speeding them past rows of cars. Carson is impressed at how efficient a driver she has become even as his daughter's cell phone rings in his pocket, even as he realizes it can only be trouble. He takes the phone out of his pocket and hits the "no" button, passes the phone back to his daughters. They are all talking at once from the backseat now. They are recommending yoga and fiber and Pilates and staying away from fats. Sick or not, they are all excellent suggestions, and one day, Carson is sure he'll think them over. For now, though, he is staring out his window from the carpool lane. They are zipping by the single commuters with their determined-looking profiles. He is thinking, *I am a man traveling back across the country to reclaim my dog*. It's not much of a thought, but there it is, taking up space and playing itself over and over in his head.

The Queen of Laundry

Carmen, the queen of laundry, was late. My mother was already back from the bay and Carmen still wasn't there. From my bed, I could smell my mother's wet suit as she padded through the living room into the bathroom. Now there was only a wall between us. I propped myself up on my elbows and picked up a book from my night table and pretended to read. I heard my mother's slight groan as she pulled the wet suit open at its seam and stepped out of it. It wasn't a full body suit; it stopped at the elbows and knees. I thought about the way it pushed her aging skin down into elaborate wrinkles of flesh at the joints and shuddered at her efficient lack of vanity.

I listened to her start the shower and lay my book flat open on the space next to me. Since my mother had been staying with me, I felt like a lazy teenager. My diagnosed depression, which once felt sturdy and reassuring, now felt faked, as if I'd placed a thermometer next to a light bulb to get out of going to school. I pulled a sweater over the leggings and T-shirt I slept in and shook Carl's leash by the front door.

He came bounding out of my daughter, Hannah's, room, where he always slept when she was gone. Hannah lived with me 50 percent of the time. The other 50 she lived with her father and his new little family. I shushed Carl, who had a tendency to bark when he saw his leash, and we took off together. Instead of feeling as if I were leaving my own house to take my dog for a walk, I felt as if I were escaping a drunken one-night stand or leaving a restaurant without paying.

When I came home an hour later, I found Carmen out front watering the thick tufts of grass in the yard. My mother's wet suit was splayed across the windshield of my car. It looked as if I had run into someone. I felt the shape of my mother's body against my windshield and sat down on the curb with Carl to get my bearings. Carmen was used to me, a white woman with way too much time on her hands, and went right on watering. It was already January, but we still didn't have any rain.

Carmen never knew what to do with my mother's wet suit. Usually she ended up stretching it out on top of the washer and dryer and scrubbing it with dish soap. Once I caught her paused with an iron over it in midair, but when she saw me, she seemed to think better of this and put the wet suit aside and moved on to one of Hannah's white school shirts.

"Pretty afternoon," I said to Carmen when I finally stood up. "You couldn't tell what was going to happen to the day this morning."

Carmen smiled and turned the water off to let me pass. She liked to work in silence, and this was fine with me, a relief from the unnecessary talk so much of the rest of the world seemed to require. I walked down the driveway past my mother's drying wet suit and smelled its familiar seaweed smell, feminine and dank. Tide, Ajax, Pine-Sol. Nothing worked. Next to the car was an empty bottle of floor polish.

"Something new," Carmen said, "to try."

I went inside, filled Carl's bowl with water and checked the January calendar sheet stuck on my refrigerator with a magnet. The librarian, Judith Redman, couldn't resist creating themes, even for the parent volunteers. Snowflakes and sleds bordered the schedule. I had lived here fifteen years now, but I still couldn't get used to the way southern Californians pretended we had weather. The calendar confirmed what I already knew, that I was up today, due at school in an hour. Every other week I checked books in and out for the third and fourth grades so I could skim my fingers over my daughter's slim knuckles for an instant during an off-week.

I let Carl out the kitchen door and found my mother sitting on a deck chair, smoking one of her clove cigarettes. Although she smoked only outside, the smell of clove lingered in her clothes and her wet hair and even mixed somehow with the smell of my own perfume. Her tubs of ground tofu spreads, her dark slices of bread, her sandy-looking unprocessed juices took up space in the refrigerator I once shared only with my daughter. I hid the boxes of orange-tinted macaroni and cheese that Hannah loved and that I only cooked in her absence, I used to tell myself, to remind me of her.

Before my mother moved in, during the weeks Hannah was with her father, I'd eat a single food all day, jasmine rice or Muenster cheese or navel oranges or tiny cinnamon hearts. Everything left me equally full and equally hungry. I experimented to find out what effect each food had on my bowels, my weight the next morning, the color of my urine.

Now my mother and I ate together each night. She cooked tofu for longevity, broccoli for our hearts and whole-wheat noodles for our colons. When Hannah was with us, my mother melted goat cheese onto her pasta shells. We had tofu pups and popsicles with no food dye or added sugars. Carl still licked our plates clean when we finished, but now when he looked up at me afterward, he looked hurt instead of grateful.

"You should have felt that water this morning," my mother said to me. She inhaled deeply and blew smoke out into the morning sky. My mother had a way of even making something like smoking look earned and righteous. "You'd know what it feels like to be alive."

Apparently, this was my problem, forgetting what it feels like to be alive. My therapist had suggested I get a roommate to help keep me on track and out of bed during the 50 percent of the time I didn't have

Hannah, and I had wound up with my mother moving in for one of her extended visits instead.

*

Although I was on time and a volunteer, the librarian always shuffled me in quickly as if I were late. "Just the yellows are left," she said today, wheeling a book cart over to me. "I already got to the blue myself while I was waiting for you." I eyed the cart she had hidden by the far side of her desk. Judith Redman didn't trust me with the Library of Congress system, just the simple alphabetical, color-coded books for the kindergarten and first-graders. I quickly shelved books about gingerbread boys and buck-toothed talking rabbits so I could be ready for check-in when my daughter's fourth-grade class lined up.

I let the return books pile up on the table while I looked for Hannah. As always, I found her in the dead center of the line. Her stepmother had parted her hair in the middle and plaited it in two braids that stopped at her shoulders, a look that was too young for her. I felt like pushing my fingers through each plait, unraveling them. I felt like weeping. "Hey, Mom," Hannah said, laying her two books on top of the growing pile. They had rules in school about affection, so I just smiled and watched her wander off to look for her two new books. I could see the place on the back of her neck where light brown hair grew in a swirled pattern. I didn't know if other mothers hungered after their children in this way. It wasn't something anyone I knew talked about, the yearning to breathe back in whole the strange bodies we had released into the world. Maybe a second child would have halved my desire, restrained it into something recognizable and polite.

"Need any help getting started there?" I heard Judith Redman say, suddenly appearing directly behind me from wherever she had been. I pointed the scanner and began checking in books. Next week Hannah was mine again.

On my way out, I stopped in the fourth-grade girl's bathroom, and, in indelible marker, wrote inside all six stall doors, *Your mother loves you, honey.* And then, in very small print, I wrote *Mrs. Redman is a bitch* in just one of them.

When I got home, my mother was washing beets at the sink, and Carmen was in the kitchen too, ironing on a tabletop pad on top of the washer and then folding laundry on top of the dryer. In the old house, she'd had her own room for the laundry, but now we all had to make do. My mother spoke to Carmen's back in the proper lispy Spanish she was studying on tape, and Carmen answered her in clipped English. Last week, Carmen had asked me how long my mother was staying and I had shrugged. First the wet suit and now this. Carmen had been with me since before Hannah was born, full-time when I was married. I got her in the divorce, but I could only afford one day a week now. Although there was nothing on paper about it, of course she came with Hannah and me.

"It's so great finally having someone native to practice with," my mother said, turning away from Carmen's back to look at me. "How was work, honey?"

"It's hardly work, Mom," I said.

"Okay, how did our little Hannah seem, then?"

I thought about my daughter with her pigtails. "She seemed like a refugee, an immigrant, a foreigner. I barely recognized her."

"Did you even touch the protein shake I made you this morning?" my mother said, scrubbing her beets aggressively now. "It would do wonders to stabilize your mood. Isn't that right, Senora Carmen?" my mother said. "Si, es correcto, no?"

Carmen shrugged her shoulders and folded my mother's flannel pajama pants down the seams, ran the iron over each leg until steam hissed above the ironing board.

*

The next morning I let my mother take me with her to the bay. We walked down the silent morning blocks, my mother in her wet suit slightly ahead of me, Carl at her heels. I stood on the beach with Carl and watched her wade into the water until it reached her chest. Then she reached her arms out in front of her and dove under, surfacing at the line of buoys the swimmers followed. *There she goes*, I thought.

Seagulls swooped past my head, and Carl barked at them. A pelican landed on a light post. *There goes my mother,* I thought.

*

At my therapy appointment, I congratulated myself on eating better and getting out of the house more. Stephanie's office smelled of exposed brick and begonias. I imagined converting it into an apartment, the kind of place I might have lived another life entirely. I vowed to fling open all of the curtains when I got home, flush down the Zoloft, chop up a fruit salad, send back my alimony check, get out a highlighter, and mark up the want ads. "I think I'm almost cured," I said.

"Can you tell me a little more about the graffiti?" she asked me.

"Really, they were more love notes," I said.

"Do you think you could have resisted the impulse if you had tried?" she asked.

I looked at the lacquered wood floor beneath my feet. It was the kind of floor that made a person want to take up tap dancing. When I got home, I'd rip out my carpets, or at least have them professionally cleaned.

"Let's pick up with that idea next Thursday," she said.

*

On Sunday afternoon, I squatted on the couch and peered under the bottom of the curtain, waiting for my ex-husband to drop off my daughter. I had a bottle of Windex in my hand in case my mother suddenly walked in the back door, fresh from the Farmer's Market with her radish roots and tomatoes on the vine, and caught me.

No one had told me about the baby until after it was born, and then Hannah told me he seemed more rat-like than human. Still, each time she came back from her 50-percent visits, I found new photos of her holding my ex-husband's new baby hidden under her homework assignment sheets on the bulletin board. I could have said something, anything, to turn this baby from something furtive into her little brother, and each time she came back from her father's I meant to do it.

I watched my daughter kiss her father's cheek and then lean over the backseat to kiss the baby. Then, I waited in my bedroom for the sound of her key turning in the front door so I wouldn't appear over-anxious to see her. *She needs to know you're okay without her,* Stephanie said. *She needs to know you exist when she's not there.*

"Carl, hey Carl," Hannah said.

"Hey, sweetie," I said. "Let me take that." While Hannah bent down to pet the dog, I picked up my daughter's backpack by a shoulder strap, key chains jangling, and gave her a kiss on the top of her head.

"We all have to get permission each time now," Hannah said, bending down lower, away from my hand. "We had to sign an honor code, and we can only go in pairs."

My hand rested in the air above my daughter's head. "I'm working on my impulse control," I said. "It's kind of the last step for me."

"Don't worry," Hannah said, taking her backpack away from me and clicking for the dog to follow her into the bedroom. "No one knows who did it."

I listened outside of her bedroom door. *What's his name?* I could ask. *Is your new brother a good sleeper?*

*

On Monday morning Carmen showed up two hours late with a plate of chicken taquitos, still steaming under the plastic wrap. She was wearing a pinafore dress that made her look like a wizened twelve-year-old. I had known her ten years and had never seen her wear anything but jeans, even at Hannah's birthday parties. "I'm sorry," Carmen said, handing me the taquitos. "You can keep the plate," she said. "It's throwaway."

"Oh, Carmen," I said. "But I got you. You're mine."

"I'm sorry. It's full-time, the way you used to be." Carmen averted her eyes, turned, and walked down the front steps. I watched her clomp down the street in white high heels that looked a size too large.

Inside the house, the laundry was waiting. My mother had taken Carl to the dog beach to run and Hannah was at school. I emptied the basket of clothes on the floor and began separating the whites from the colors. Before my marriage, I did this all the time, but now I was crippled with decisions, pastels and neons and rough cotton blends. *You have a college degree,* I told myself. *You can figure this out.*

*

At the winter parent volunteer luncheon, I pulled my beige skirt down closer to my kneecaps. I had shaved up to them but not over them, and they looked hairy in the gleaming sunlight of the playground. My skirt had shrunk in the wash. Probably it was the kind of skirt a person usually wore pantyhose with anyway. Probably it should have been hand-washed, in cold water. All around me, mothers were dressed in peg-legged pants and ironed jeans. Their buffed toenails gleamed in their sandals. They compared notes on their children's math tutors, lowering their voices and smiling whenever one of the children who were waiting on us neared our table. Their voices collapsed in the air around me.

For dessert, our children served us chocolate pudding designed to look like dirt in the base of baked graham-cracker flowerpots. I pulled out my paper flower, put my napkin on the table, and faked a small wave at my daughter who was now waiting on a distant table. She had taken five years of ballet, had never missed a class, but wasn't invited to solo at her recitals. She wasn't graceful as she poured refills of iced tea, but anyone could see her earnestness. Was my daughter supposed to have a math tutor, too? What did I know anymore?

The inside doors of the fourth-grade bathroom stalls had been painted over in a shade of gray that didn't quite match the rest of the walls. *Impulse control,* I wrote on the inside of just one of them in neat, careful script, and then I walked home.

*

In my house, I found my mother listening to bluegrass. Still in her wet suit from her morning swim, she flicked her feather duster around the living room furniture. When she saw me, she turned down the volume. The moment felt almost familiar, as if Carmen had turned off the vacuum cleaner to let me pass. My mother smiled her distracted, busy smile and aimed her feather duster at a picture frame.

— 27

I walked through the kitchen and out back through the yard to the garage. I found the tiny purple wading pool Hannah used to swim in when she was a toddler and that no one had ever bought at any of our yearly yard sales. It was full of black bugs. I centered the pool in the yard, turned on the hose, and watched the bugs scurry out over the sides. Carl came out and started to lap at the water as if I'd filled a large dog bowl.

"So, did you mothers feel properly applauded?" my mother asked from the back door, the feather duster by her side.

"They made us corkscrew salad," I said. "It was very pleasant."

"I'd forgotten how satisfying housework can be," my mother said.

A Goodyear blimp floated overhead. My mother and I watched its slow-motion flight.

Two Parties

Even though it's only nine-thirty when Victoria's family arrives at Lagoon Park to claim tables, the good ones—the ones on the sun-side of the playground—are already taken. A man sits at each. They can see this when they pull up, before they even get out of the car. "Perfect," Victoria's mother says. Because it's her birthday, Victoria sits in front between her mother and father, instead of in the backseat of their Escort. She's had to duck at each intersection on the way here so a policeman wouldn't stop her father and make her belt up in the back.

Her mother and father tape down paper Lion King tablecloths while Victoria, in her tight, shiny shoes, climbs a slide and feels the wind up her dress. One of the men at the good tables tries to light a cigarette but gives up.

"It's just the marine layer. I'm not worried," her father says, eyeing the sky.

Victoria sits on top of the slide and looks at her mother after her father speaks. All morning her mother has been angry-busy. Now she is using liters of soda as paperweights, slamming them into the corners of their two tables, even though her parents have already taped down the tablecloths. Later, there will be too many bubbles. Her mother had wanted to have Victoria's party in a restaurant this year, but her father had said, *Where's the money coming from?*

Flinging out her arms as if for balance, Victoria walks across the ramp that connects all the slides. This park has no swings, and Victoria's girlfriends from pre-K like only swings, not slides. Victoria thinks about pushing them one by one off this ramp if they complain. She thinks about sand in their faces and up their underpants and about being the only clean one left.

She sits on top of the slide that faces the tables that were supposed to be hers. One of the men looks up from a crossword puzzle he's doing in a newspaper that's curling up in the wind. "How old are you going to be?" Victoria asks him.

"Ha!" he says and shouts to the man at the next table, "She thinks it's my birthday."

The other man has his arms folded on the table and his head down like when it's quiet time at pre-K.

Victoria hears her mother shouting for her to come back over there and squeezes her legs shut and slides down. She walks past the man who laughed at her and sticks her tongue out at him before turning and running toward her parents.

"Do you want a sandwich while you're waiting for your friends?" her mother says.

On the table are two huge jars, one full of peanut butter, the other the wrong kind of jelly, the red instead of the purple. At least the bread is white, not brown.

"We're doing a make-your-own-sandwich-bar," her father says. "Won't that be fun?"

"Christ," her mother says, rooting through a Costco box, "you forgot the utensils. What next?"

*

Because there are no utensils, Victoria's pre-K friends suck on peanut-butter-covered fingers. They poke eye slots in the bread, chew gaping mouth holes, and growl at each other through their bread masks. This is a drop-off party and her parents are the only adults who stay to watch them. At school, they would all be in time-out for playing with their food instead of eating it, but her father makes his own bread mask and joins right in, growling a little too loudly. Victoria's mother is sitting in the car with her coat zipped tight, smoking a cigarette. Through her bread mask, Victoria can see her mother behind the windshield and is relieved to find her in the passenger's seat, not the driver's.

Holding her bread mask to her face, Victoria leaves her friends growling at her father, climbs up a slide and tiptoes across the platform. The other party has started now, too. Except for one boy, who's wearing a leather jacket too large for him, there are only grown-ups at this party. They're drinking cans of soda and looking off at the lagoon as if they expect something to rise out of it. Victoria chews on her bread mask and watches the boy drag a stick through the sand, writing letters. Even on the sun-side of the park, there's no sun. *S U C K*, Victoria reads each letter to herself. She knows her letters but only a few words: *Mom* and *Dad* and *Stop* and, of course, *Victoria*.

The boy looks up at Victoria and says, "What's your problem?"

Her mouth is full of bread and peanut butter, and when she tries to say something smart back to him, she can't talk. She wonders if she's gagging and will die on her fifth birthday here at Lagoon Park, but then she swallows and she's okay. "You," she says. "You're my problem."

"Good one," the boy says and goes back to his stick writing.

*

When the pizza delivery car pulls up to Lagoon Park, all of Victoria's pre-K friends go running over to it. Victoria looks at her father who shrugs back at her. She looks in the car for her mother but doesn't see her behind the windshield anymore. The pizza delivery boy wears a red cap and shirt. He holds the boxes up high in the air and looks around over the girls' heads. An adult from the other side of the park walks toward the boy, counting out the bills in his hand, and takes the pizzas away. The girls follow after him and so does Victoria.

"Who shorted me?" the man says. "Who's not with the program here?"

"Looks like you picked up some little chickens, too," the man who laughed at Victoria in the morning says.

Victoria decides to call the man who laughs Chicken Man in her head. She feels the expectant bodies of her friends from the pre-K all around her, their cold bare legs in their dresses, their arms wrapped around their chests. "I thought we were supposed to have lunch at your party," one of them says. "My mom said you were serving lunch."

"Come on, girls, take a load off," Chicken Man says. "We'll throw you a crust."

Victoria and her girlfriends sit at one of the tables that were supposed to be hers. She looks over at the Lion King tables for her father's permission, but he's gone now, too.

"I don't like anything on it," one of her friends says.

"I only like it plain, too," says another friend.

"Ha!" says Chicken Man. "It looks as if our little sobriety celebration has been graced by princesses."

Chicken Man serves Victoria and her friends pizza on thin napkins. Victoria feels mushroom stems in her mouth, oily bits of onion, sour meat. She thinks this is the best thing she has ever tasted in her life. She finishes off her slice quickly and looks around at her friends who are still picking off the toppings and wipes her hands clean on her party dress. *I am five,* she thinks. *I am the birthday girl.*

After they eat, Chicken Man and the boy chase Victoria and her friends around the playground. Chicken Man wheezes and has to stop to catch his breath but the boy keeps going. Victoria's friends run up the slides and screech. The boy seems to be after all of them at once, but Chicken Man is after only Victoria. She hides under a slide and he grabs her around the middle and tickles her under the arms. She feels his hand move between her legs, outside and then inside her panties. "Getting out the sand," he whispers, before letting her go.

Victoria hears her mother calling them over and runs back to the Lion King tables.

"Who's your friend?" her father says, lifting a white cake out of a grocery store box.

Victoria looks around. The boy from the other party is there with her pre-K friends, waiting for cake. Her mother is smiling now, and she serves each of them pieces that are too large to eat. "I can't believe my sweetheart is a big five-year-old already," her mother says, cupping Victoria's face in her hands.

They have forgotten to sing to her, and it's too late for that now. Victoria's presents are piled on the ground. She can't remember what she asked for, what she wanted.

The boy tosses his cake plate in the garbage bag her father has set out and says "later" and walks back to his side of the park.

Victoria sits at a table with her girlfriends. Victoria's parents stand holding hands, watching the girls eat. "We took a little walk around the lagoon while you girls were playing," her father says. "We remembered the night we made you and got straight with our priorities."

One of Victoria's friends giggles, and another says to pretend the frosting is shaving cream. Her friends make frosting shaving cream goatees. The cake has no taste but Victoria eats anyway. She makes her goatee and then, for her parents' sake, she swallows, first one bite and then another.

Fumes

At four o'clock, it was mostly nannies that remained at the tot lot, Hispanic and Filipino women that Walden had come to recognize as regulars. They ignored the children and each other, each lost in what looked to Walden like his own familiar gloom. The children appeared oblivious to the prevailing mood of the late summer afternoon and chased each other with energetic rancor around the playground's fenced-in perimeter.

All the children, that is, except two little girls with elaborate, multicolored ribbons in their thin blond hair, who sat under the shade of the plastic slide, sifting sand onto each other's knees and whispering. He'd seen them here before. Sisters, he assumed. He squinted and finally located their mother smoking a cigarette just outside the tot lot gate. She wore a T-shirt tucked up under her bra and tight sweatshorts that Walden could see, even from this distance, had inched their way into the crevice of her buttocks. This woman, whom he had observed for the past several days, seemed pathetic yet desirable in a private, limited kind of way to Walden, unlike his wife, Ellen, who, with her neatly trimmed fingernails and soft lilac fragrance, had always been much closer to the kind of woman he fantasized about sitting across from in a restaurant during his long single days.

One of the nannies had taken over more than her share of the bench by spreading out a diaper bag, juice boxes, fruit rolls, and several children's sweatshirts. She fanned her magazine aggressively in the air in the direction of the cigarette smoke behind her head until the blond woman finally stepped back a foot, stubbed out her cigarette and shouted, "Come on, girls! Let's get a move on."

Walden turned and headed back in the direction of his own cul-de-sac. As he neared the corner, he heard the blond woman's staticky car radio blaring over the grinding sound of her defective muffler, but he didn't turn around to look until he was certain she had nearly reached the cement columns that marked the entrance to El Covino Estates. Then he watched her silver Honda take a too-sharp right.

For the past three days, Walden had been slowly cleaning out his house. When he got home from work at three-thirty, the early shift at Boeing, he carried as many items as he could take in one trip down the hill to his mother's garage, then walked back home, the muscles in his calves aching from the unfamiliar exertion. Although his biceps felt huge, when he looked in a mirror he saw little improvement.

Walden unlocked his front door, entered his partially dissembled living room, and, for the first time, had to admit that Ellen had a point. With the end tables gone and the stereo stripped to its most useful functions, the room did seem slightly larger now, although he frankly wondered what difference this would ultimately make since any potential buyers would certainly be familiar with their second-rate floor plan if they knew the development at all. Two years ago, they purchased one of the less expensive, early starter models without the cathedral ceilings, and it seemed obvious now to Walden that no amount of emptying out would fool anyone into thinking otherwise.

"Hello!" he called out, although he knew he was alone, trying for an echo effect that failed. Feeling his voice being absorbed into the carpet, he walked into the kitchen.

Walden took a beer out of the refrigerator, slid open the back door, and, instead of appreciating the small vista of his well-maintained backyard the way he once did, listened to the chronic buzz of traffic on the 405 freeway, exactly one-quarter of a mile north. The truth was that he had grown up with this sound and so never really heard it until Ellen pointed it out to him, which she did shortly after they had moved into the house.

When they first saw the house, still newlyweds then, the central air-conditioning had created a reassuring, familiar purr that had effectively blocked any outside sounds, even as they stood in the backyard and imagined where they would dig the posts for the cedar swing set they planned to buy as soon as Ellen became pregnant. Ellen claimed later to have mistaken the buzz of freeway traffic for the new Rudd unit the previous owners had installed.

Now she blamed Walden. Who could fault her? He grew up here. Why hadn't he warned her, she wanted to know. Walden knew his own explanation seemed fraudulent, even if it was the truth. He hadn't ever noticed how close the freeway was, although he had spent the greater part of his life living in El Covino Estates, just one long block from here.

To his credit, he reasoned, it wasn't the kind of noise you had to shout over to be heard. The only trucks that rumbled down the quiet cul-de-sacs carried bottles of water for home coolers and an occasional new couch from Mervyns. Children were trusted to ride their bikes in these streets until just after dark in the summer, where, on some warm Saturdays during his mostly dull adolescence, Walden had felt so hemmed in by the familiar sound of nothing happening outside his bedroom window that he'd longed for a motorcycle gang to ride through, leaving angry black stripes on the carefully maintained roads. If he had heard the freeway traffic at all, it would have probably given him a sense a possibility, that there was somewhere else to go and a lot of people already on their way. But even as a bored teenager, he realized he was lucky to grow up in El Covino Estates, and that his children would be lucky to grow up here, too.

But, of course, his children, if he ever had any, would not now grow up in El Covino Estates. "It's this place," she told Walden, gently rubbing her flat abdomen, shortly after her miscarriage. "It's like living in a toxic waste dump. All those fluorocarbons in the air. Not to mention the rubber from all those tires. Just thousands of little rubber particles floating through the air every minute. No wonder this baby wanted out."

But what had really convinced Ellen of the necessity to move was her sister's breast cancer support group. Not that her sister lived anywhere near the 405. She lived across the country, in Maine, where Walden had never been but where he imagined the air was pure and clear enough to hold up against even the worst freeway traffic exhaust fumes. But her sister had joined a cancer support group that emphasized environmental factors in the development of lymph nodes, and hanging up the phone with her one Sunday, Ellen had told him she had come to a decision. If he still wanted a future with her, they would have to put the house on the market.

The first two realtors they interviewed, both petite, perfectly made up women who Walden couldn't help but notice even Ellen looked slightly shabby next to, took only a perfunctory tour of the house, claiming to already know the model well. Then they all returned to the living room, where each delicately asked what price they had hoped to get for their home, before talking about the stagnant market, spreading comps out on the coffee table, and dismissing their absurd notions.

The third realtor, a jovial man who wore red suspenders over a white dress shirt, lingered in each room during the house tour, opening closets and admiring their organization and shelf space. When they were finally through with that, instead of pulling out the same comps Walden had readied himself for, he turned the pages of a large loose-leaf notebook full of laminated pages of his award certificates and letters of appreciation. While the realtor discussed his achievements, Walden glanced periodically at Ellen, hoping to discern her attitude toward him, hoping this would be the one she'd accept, and they could go back to spending their weeknights playing long games of Scrabble and watching the old movie channel on cable the way they used to before they had begun inviting perfect strangers into their home.

But instead she surprised him by not choosing any of them. "FiSBO," she said to him the morning after they had interviewed the third realtor. "For Sale By Owner," she clarified when he looked at her, confused. "I was thinking, we should just go on ahead and sell it ourselves."

Walden had never sold anything in his life, unless he counted the time in eighth grade when he sold chocolate bars to raise money for a class trip to Washington, D.C., and even then he wasn't very good at it, giving neighbors random discounts when they didn't have the full five dollars handy. And now his wife expected him to help her sell an entire house.

She had even signed up for a four-day FiSBO seminar in Big Bear—this is where she was now—which, as best as Walden could tell from the brochure, was run by retired and disenchanted realtors. The entire brochure struck Walden as falsely upbeat and second-rate with its constant appeal to a capital *YOU, TOO*, but Ellen had insisted she had checked references and these people knew what they were doing.

*

When the phone rang, Walden knew it would be Ellen with more instructions on this Sunday's open house. He decided to let the machine answer it, so he wouldn't be forced to ask questions and take notes. Already, he was certain he had missed several important areas of concern. For example, just yesterday she had urgently asked him to do something to the bathroom besides clean it, but now he couldn't remember what. Repaint, maybe? But then, what color?

Better to have it all on tape. From the doorway to the back yard, he listened to his wife's voice fill their kitchen. It amazed him that she could talk for entire sentences this way without getting any response. He walked back into the yard and pushed at a slightly buckled rail in the wood fence that didn't budge. Behind the fence, the neighbors' mock tree house—really just a wood platform with an old steering wheel bolted onto it—loomed. Like his own yard, theirs was flat and free of actual trees.

*

On Sunday morning, Walden made a point of getting up as soon as he first felt himself stir to make his final preparations for the open house, instead of pursuing his customary weekend ritual of turning over in the direction of where his wife usually slept, fluffing up his pillow and falling back to sleep for another hour. He had slept without her for the past three nights now and had begun to get used to it. For dinner he ate chili dogs and powdered donuts from the 7-11, and last night even fell asleep without first brushing his teeth. He felt as if he were living alone again, but this time with the strength of a fallback position—Ellen—which made his present reality much more pleasant than his actual, often anxiety-ridden, single life had been.

He had managed to speak to Ellen only once in the past three days, assuring her he had been spending his time buying touch-up paint, brighter light bulbs, and spring bouquet room deodorizer, all according to her specifications. She had seemed dubious but let it go when he assured her all would be ready and that he had even, on his own, placed an additional ad for their open house in a free paper that he had come across in the 7-11.

It was one of Ellen's latest ideas that the open house should include Walden serving beverages. Specifically, by noon, Walden was to be dressed in his beige suit and prepared to greet each potential buyer with champagne served in a long-stemmed fluted plastic glass, just purchased yesterday at a party supply outlet off the 110. Walden was not thrilled with the idea of wearing a suit on a Sunday in his own home, but knew his wife planned to return by three from her seminar and didn't want her to be disappointed so added this detail to his accumulated list.

At 11:45 Walden stood in front of his house and surveyed the property, the eighteenth and final task on the list he accumulated from her phone calls over the past several days. "Final Survey of Property Site," he read, and stepped back a few feet for a better look. Not sure exactly what he was supposed to be surveying for, Walden decided to straighten out the brass mailbox by the front door, which, it seems to him, had always hung slightly to the left. He adjusted it and then watched it slide back down again. Apparently, this would take nails or at least a screwdriver, which Walden had no time for if he was supposed to be showered and dressed in fifteen minutes. Stepping carefully around the new "Welcome" doormat—number nine on his "to do" list—Walden checked off the eighteenth and final item and went back inside.

By twelve-thirty, although showered and dressed, Walden was still alone. He felt something was vaguely wrong, as if he were about to be caught waiting for his own surprise party. Unfamiliar classical music played softly in the background as Walden straightened out the stack of fact sheets he had made up about the house and practiced getting up casually from the living room couch and thrusting out his hand to shake the hands of imaginary "guests." Ellen said thinking of them this way would make him more hospitable. Walden was to be their host, at least until Ellen got home, when she would become the hostess, and, presumably, he could take a break from his hosting duties.

Walden checked his appearance in the downstairs powder room one more time. His hair was slicked back in a style he had copied out of the Sunday Magazine section, and he was hoping he didn't look as bug-eyed and foolish as he now appeared to himself. Feeling slightly nauseated from the smell of spring bouquet room deodorizer, Walden took a detour to the kitchen and opened one of ten chilled bottles of champagne that waited in a picnic cooler on the counter before resuming his perch on the living room couch.

When the door that had been left purposely slightly ajar swung fully open at two o'clock, Walden had consumed four glasses of champagne and hosted three guests. Two, who on second thought did look vaguely familiar to Walden, turned out to be neighbors from three doors over. Evasive and somewhat hostile finally, the couple had refused Walden's numerous attempts to offer them champagne, and had only signed the register when Walden practically blocked their attempt to head back out the front door without first doing so. The third guest turned out to be a realtor, who, after accepting Walden's champagne and drinking it as quickly as if it were a shot of rye, handed him her card and told him that when he got tired of trying to do this on his own to give her a call.

Slightly wary now, Walden rose from the couch a bit more slowly this time, a glass of champagne ready in hand, and approached the front door. "Welcome!" he said, trying to muster up his enthusiasm.

At first he didn't quite recognize her, which is the way it usually went with Walden when a person surprised him by appearing out of context. It wasn't only neighbors, either. Once it took him the better part of an hour-long weekend shuttle he and Ellen took to Las Vegas to figure out that the man who periodically smiled at him from across the aisle worked just five cubicles away from him in the same office.

"Is the lady of the house home?" the woman who stood in front of him now asked. She was wearing a blue flowered dress with the kind of small rounded collar Walden expected to see on someone much younger than she appeared to be. Walden guessed her age as thirty-five, then subtracted two years for the harsh sunlight, which magnified the split ends of her blond hair.

"No, no, but do come in," Walden said. "I'll be your host today."

"Whatever." The woman lifted up a thick black case that Walden failed to notice was resting on the stoop next to her and followed him into the house. "Tell me," she asked. "What would you say is your worst cleaning problem?"

"Excuse me?" Walden said.

"Brass? Doorknobs are often it. Kitchen floor? Bathtub ring?" She took a seat on the couch and, much to Walden's dismay, heaved her black suitcase onto the just dusted coffee table, apparently oblivious to the fact that she was covering, and probably permanently damaging, his carefully stacked fact sheets.

"Got kids?" she asked, looking around. "Doesn't matter. Biodegradable is good for you and me, too. Good for our environment. And all that jazz. Etcetera. Etcetera."

Walden watched her begin setting plastic bottles upright that had been fastened to the inside of her suitcase. She unscrewed the cap to a clear bottle, pulled out the thin wand that attached to the spray nozzle, then stuck out her tongue and ran the wand over it. "Tastes like lemonade. Minus the sugar, of course" she said, licking her lips for emphasis. "Completely natural, like all of our products. Come worst-case scenario—earthquake, flood, what have you—you could drink the stuff if you had to. Not that we actually endorse that, of course."

"I think there's been a mistake here," Walden said. "I'm really not in the market for any cleaning products. In fact, just the opposite. I'm having an open house today. We hope to sell the place, not clean it."

"You're leaving? Man, I'd buy your house if I could. Who would ever want to move from here? My kids and me, we love this neighborhood. All single-family. None of those damn complexes where every minute you've got some teenager blasting his music right onto your balcony." She sighed, stood up, screwed the lid back on the bottle, and then adjusted her dress, which had begun to sneak into the crevice of her buttocks. Suddenly Walden remembered where he'd seen her.

"Do you take them to the playground here? Your kids?"

"Sure," she said. "I like the way it's all fenced in and everything, and, really, you get a better quality of people at it than you do where we live, if you know what I mean. Nice kids. Not real pushy and filthy-mouthed the way they are some places. You have kids? Because it doesn't look that way to me. Ha! This place looks barely lived in."

"No. Not yet, I mean," Walden said. "I just sometimes walk by the tot lot on the way home from my mother's." Walden felt the remaining energy begin to fade from the afternoon as he tried to explain how it happened that he'd seen her. It was now 2:10, and he had not yet had one real potential buyer show up. "Were you serious about wanting to buy the place?" Walden asked, remembering his wife explaining something about creative financing on one of her messages. "Maybe we can work something out. Do you have any down payment at all?"

"If fifty dollars can get me in the door, and you can find a lender that doesn't know how to spell bad credit."

"Oh," Walden said. "Probably that's a no, then."

"Yeah. So's anyway," she said, snapping her suitcase shut. "Nice meeting you. Good luck and all that good stuff."

Walden watched her pick up her suitcase, his crumbled fact sheets fanning out across the table. "Do you want a glass of champagne?" he asked, remembering the glass he still held in his hand. "It's for everyone," he said, "who comes by to look at the house." He almost added that this was his wife's idea, but decided against mentioning it.

"If I get some orange juice mixed in with it. Because a girl gets awfully thirsty lugging this stuff around all day, I can me tell you that. And it's no picnic licking that wand every ten minutes even if the stuff is supposedly harmless."

In the kitchen, Walden poured out half the glass of champagne, replacing it with orange juice and two ice cubes. As an afterthought, he added a sprig of parsley.

"Yeah, real nice place. Thanks," she said, accepting the drink. "Melanie Thorton," she said, putting the drink down on the coffee table and extending her right hand.

"Walden," he said. "Walden Berryman." It was only recently that Walden had begun to learn to say his last name without mumbling. As if being named Walden wasn't bad enough, *Berryman* had made his name a double source of aggravation for him well through high school. Growing up he had to endure being called alternately Waldo the Strawberry Man, the Raspberry Man, and, somehow worst of all, the Boysenberry Man. He trusted this woman who sat in front of him now, this Melanie Thorton who had two kids she supported in this less than glamorous way, to be mature enough not to comment.

"Is Mr. Thorton in sales, too?" he asked, feeling emboldened by his relative position of power: his house, his living room, his champagne, his orange juice.

"Mr. Thorton? Ha! That's a good one. In sales. Yeah, I guess you could say he was. Now he's mostly in jail."

"Oh, I'm sorry."

"Hardly your fault. Anyways. Seeing how my kids are probably crawling all over the car by now, I'd better be moving on to the next house."

"Your children are in the car?" Walden thought about an article he read just last week about a woman leaving her two Pomeranians in the car with the windows cracked while she went into Ralph's to pick up a baked chicken for dinner only to discover them dead from heat exhaustion when she came back out. What kind of woman left her kids alone in the car this long? He was certain if Ellen ever did decide to try to have children again, she wouldn't be this kind of mother.

"It's not easy, you know," Melanie said as if reading his thoughts. "Being a single mother and all. I do the best I can."

"I didn't mean to imply anything," Walden said. "I was just thinking it must be getting kind of warm out there. Do you want to invite them in for some juice first?" Walden was sure that something about wearing this ridiculous suit, being the *host* of a party that did not seem to be materializing was changing him into a much more polite person than he intended to be. Despite his invitation, with the same urgency he had wanted this woman to stay, he now wanted her to leave.

"Well, sure, for a minute would be fine. That's very decent of you to ask." Melanie opened the front door and shouted out "Girls!" to her children in a voice that Walden was sure echoed throughout his cul-de-sac.

He walked into the kitchen and quickly filled two plastic champagne glasses with juice. He envisioned handing the children their glasses before they sat down and then making an excuse about having to get back to work. But when he came back into the living room, they were already seated side by side next to their mother on the couch, wearing matching light blue short sets and the same elaborate ribbons he recognized from the playground. Classical music droned on in the background.

"Say 'thank you' to the nice man, girls," their mother said. But they just stared at him while they sipped.

He remembered them whispering together conspiratorially under the slide and decided he didn't like them any better than their mother. "Say, do you girls want to come out back and see something pretty terrific?" he asked.

They looked at their mother and, opening her suitcase again, she shooed them with the back of her hand and told them to go on ahead. "I'm just going to give you a little demonstration of our cleaning products while you're gone since you've been so nice. I see your dining room table over there could use a little scuff-proofing and shining. Etcetera, etcetera. You'll see. You'll hardly recognize it when you get back."

Walden felt the girls following him through the kitchen out to the backyard. They walked as softly as people who might be planning a sneak attack. Walden made a mental note to be sure to tell his own future children always to make their presence fully known. The buzz of the freeway felt as persistent as the thick summer air itself against his suit this afternoon. How could he have ever been so dense as to not notice it? "See," Walden says, pointing to the neighbors' raised playhouse. "What do you girls think of that?"

"Cool," the taller one said flatly. "Can we go in it?" Before Walden could stop her, she bent down and lifted her sister up until she was able to grab onto the top of the fence and hoist herself onto the wood platform of the mock tree house. Then, lifting her foot into the air, she told Walden to give her a boost. "Fold them together and put your hands out flat," she said. "Palms up."

Against his better judgment, Walden did as he was told. He felt her light, sneakered foot in the palm of his hands and readied himself for her full weight, which turned out to be less than he expected.

"You can go back inside now," the older girl told him. "Maybe bring us out some cookies later."

"Oreos are our favorite," the younger one added.

"Our mom's friends usually buy them for us," the older one said. "Or at least Fig Newtons."

Walden was at a loss. Any minute now his wife would be driving up. He had five bottles of champagne left and had given away none of his photocopied fact sheets. A strange woman was shining the dining room table his wife had inherited from her grandmother. He looked up at the girls, who had settled into their new roost with their knees folded up against their chests. The bright bows in their hair suddenly looked as exotic to him as peacocks' feathers.

He grabbed hold of the top of the fence and hoisted himself up, feeling his pant leg catch on a nail. For two full years, he had never seen anyone in this tree house. These neighbors either didn't have any children or, if they did, they had grown up and moved away.

As far as Walden was concerned, there was plenty of room for the three of them in the mock tree house, but the girls huddled tightly together under the steering wheel as he pulled himself up and then kneeled down beside them. Off in the distance, a dog barked.

"Most of them don't really play with us, Mister," the taller one said. "We're kind of used to playing alone. Mostly, they get us cookies or once in a while drop us off at a movie."

"Obviously," Walden said, "I am not like most men. Who wants to pretend we're pirates, waiting for the fair wench to appear so we can ambush her?"

"I don't think that's a nice thing to call our mom," the smaller one said. "Is it, Ashley?"

Ashley shrugged her shoulders. "Whatever. We don't want to play that game with you. Get it?"

"Come have a look-see," Melanie yelled out through the back door, then took a drag off her cigarette and continued to talk while the smoke wafted out of her mouth. "I took that old, dark layer right off that table. You'll hardly recognize it. Come on. Where are you hiding?"

He watched her squint into his backyard, survey his carefully tended juniper bushes, his border of flowering jasmine. There was obviously no place for them to hide. "Shh," he whispered to the girls. "Let's make her really look." He felt them nudge each other and sink down lower.

"I mean it, girls," she yelled, stepping out into the yard now and blowing smoke up into the sky.

"Ho, matey," Walden yelled back. "Look up here. At the pirate ship."

He watched her finally locate them.

"You come on out of that thing right now, girls. Shouldn't you, too, Mr. Burlyman?"

"Weirdo," Ashley whispered to him as she helped lift her sister before climbing down herself.

Walden climbed down slowly, careful not to rip the other pant leg. He heard his wife's voice calling out and thought about climbing back up, but it was too late. Both women were in the backyard now, watching him, the children already having gone back inside. Walden wiped his palms against the front of his pants and tried out a broad bon vivant smile that he felt went well with his suit and hairstyle.

Ellen had done something to her own hair while she was away. Her thin bangs, which he now saw he had come to rely upon laying smoothly over her forehead, had been gelled up into a sharp-looking little crest.

"I see you two already met," he said.

"Not really," Ellen said, folding her arms over her chest. And then, as if she had just remembered her own lecture about "guests," she uncrossed them and extended a hand to Melanie. "A pleasure to meet you. I hope you're enjoying the house."

"I was just showing her kids the yard, honey," Walden said.

"Ah, the yard," Ellen said, squinting out skeptically into the afternoon around them. "Yes, great for kids. Lots of room to roam."

"Mr. Burlyman, Mrs. Burylman, you too, stop yabbering and come on in here and see what I've done for your table," Melanie said.

"Table?" Ellen said.

Walden shrugged at Ellen and followed Melanie and his wife back inside through the kitchen into the dining area of the living room, where Ellen's grandmother's table sat looking raw and gleaming, peeled of its skin.

"You ruined it," Ellen said, rubbing her fingers over its new shining surface. "Who is this woman? She ruined my table. Is she even interested in buying our house, Walden?"

"You don't have to get nasty," Melanie said. "I was trying to do you all a favor. Normally this product—all biodegradable ingredients, too, I might add, Mr. Burlyman—would run you fifteen dollars before taxes." She put the cap back on an opened bottle and then snapped shut her black suitcase. "Girls, come on out wherever you are. We better get a move on."

They filed silently out of the powder room, Ellen's shade of peach lipstick applied neatly to their mouths, and walked out the front door with their mother.

"Jesus, Walden," Ellen said. She shook her head at the table, and then walked upstairs with her overnight bag. "It's a good thing I got home when I did," she shouted down to him.

The powder room still smelled of spring bouquet room deodorizer, but the hand towels he had washed and hung with the borders facing downward were now wrinkled and mis-hung. He straightened them out as best he could and looked in the bathroom mirror to see how his new hairstyle was holding up. The girls had written the word *Butthed* with Ellen's lipstick across the glass. The misspelling solidified his dislike for them. He smudged the word with several sheets of toilet paper and then gave up.

Walden walked out across his backyard and climbed up into the neighbor's tree house again. He knew he should come down and talk to his wife about her weekend, but Walden didn't want to. Not yet anyway. Instead, he steadied himself and stood on the platform, his feet planted firmly apart. Like a ship's captain, he shaded his eyes with his hand before boldly looking off in the horizon, waiting to see just what surprises were in store for him next.

Indoor-Outdoor Pool

Royce spent as much of his shared vacation as he could swimming between the outdoor and indoor pools at the hotel. While his parents, who hadn't lived together since before Royce was born, read their novels on lounge chairs, he developed a kind of underwater twist-turn that felt to him both graceful and efficient. At seven, he hadn't yet completely ruled out the possibility of mermaids, and, in the creation of his twist-turn, he emulated what he imagined to be their technique, a flick of the tail, or, in his case, legs pressed tightly together like a tail. He wished his mother's boyfriend, Chris, were here to see this because he was the only adult Royce knew who might truly appreciate the maneuver.

If Royce took enough breath beforehand, he could twist-turn three times before coming up for air. In which pool he surfaced—the indoor or the outdoor—involved a kind of math that Royce hadn't yet mastered. It seemed likely to be an addition problem, but Royce wouldn't bet on it.

Math was his worst subject, although Royce liked the idea of it a lot, and sometimes the very best part of the day at school involved sitting on the rug and watching his teacher's chalk stick skim along the board, adding up and taking away. His teacher had gotten them to write about their lives in journals all year long, but Royce felt math would have made more sense for this particular project. As he completed his third twist-turn, he made up a problem in his head. Breakfast plus swimming plus lunch plus swimming plus dinner plus cable TV minus bed equals tomorrow.

Each year of his life for as long as he could remember equaled the same addition problem: fall plus spring with his mother; Christmas plus summer with his father. And this in-between week with them both, which now seemed to him possibly to require fractions, a foggy concept his first-grade teacher introduced only a few weeks before school let out. She had used a toy pizza in her demonstration, its slices stuck together with Velcro, and, in Royce's opinion, appeared to be bewildered by the concept herself.

Royce surfaced in the dim light of the indoor pool, which was full of babies this morning, bobbing around in yellow floaties, their mothers smiling madly at them. He looked up at the empty lounge chairs and felt confused, then remembered that his parents were reading by the outside pool. They both liked heat and sun, and, during this in-between week, their hair smelled dry and mushroomy. Although he knew better, Royce liked to think of his parents as brother and sister. They even looked vaguely alike, with their reddish suntans and rounded shoulders. Royce made a silly face at the baby nearest him, dove under, and resurfaced in the screaming light of the outside pool. The lifeguard's seat was perched high above this pool, and Royce looked up at his white visor and mirrored sunglasses as his eyes adjusted.

"There's our boy!" Royce's father shouted out to him as Royce climbed up the underwater ladder.

"You mean our dolphin," Royce's mom said.

"Half boy, half dolphin, what would that make you Royce?" his father asked as his mother edged herself down to the end of her lounge chair and wrapped a towel around him.

Although the question sounded friendly enough—even silly—Royce knew that this was a trick question, one of his father's tests to see if he was learning anything at the hippie school his mother sent him to in Tacoma Park. "Dolphboy?" Royce said.

"Or?" his father asked.

Royce thought for a moment, then tried the word in his head before saying it aloud. "Boydolph?"

"Or?" his father asked.

"Okay, that's enough," his mother said. "I thought this was supposed to be a vacation, not summer school."

"It's just a game, Charlotte," his father said. "We were having fun, weren't we, kiddo?"

"Can I have money for the candy machine?" Royce said.

The candy machine was a kind of trick question, too. If you pushed the wrong letter-number combinations, you could end up with peppermint Lifesavers instead of an Almond Joy. Still, it was better than standing here watching his parents begin to start up one of their in-between week arguments. Both his parents reached for their wallets, which sat next to each other on the glass-covered table between their lounge chairs, but his father won. "Knock yourself out, buddy," he said, handing Royce a dollar bill.

Barefoot, Royce walked the length of the pool, waiting for a moment when he reached the inside part for his eyes to adjust from the sunlight, and then down three steps to the candy machine. A boy he had noticed the day before in the gift shop was playing one of the two video games next to the vending machines. He imagined putting his arms around the boy's waist and hugging him close, breathing in whatever he might smell like, but instead he said, "Excuse me," and stepped around him to reach the candy machine. Royce wished his mother had gotten to her wallet first because it had a change purse, and she would have given him four quarters. He lined up his father's dollar bill carefully, following the diagram on the machine and let the machine take its time sucking it in. It came back anyway, and Royce sighed and began to try again.

"Fucking sucks that machine," the boy said to him, turning from his video game. "Here, let me do it for you." The boy folded the bill the long way down the middle and pulled the fingers of his other hand tight across it. Royce worried he would rip his father's dollar, but instead he unfolded a flat bill, which the machine swallowed.

"Cool," Royce said. He stood on his toes to fully examine his choices, pushed the combination that he hoped would give him a Twix with its neat seam down the middle, so he could offer half to the boy. But by the time it came out and he had reached under the plastic lip of the machine to retrieve it, the boy was already back at his game.

"Want to play?" he said, not taking his eyes off the screen where bursts of gunfire were erupting.

Royce shook his head, and then, realizing the boy couldn't see him even though he was standing next to him, said, "Nah, you go ahead." Although many of the kids in his class seemed to know a lot about video games, Royce didn't know anything. In Royce's mother's house they didn't even have a television, and he knew that if he asked his father for a PlayStation, his father would find a way to turn it into something educational.

Royce took both halves of his Twix and walked back to the outdoor pool. His father's lounge chair was empty. His mother was still in her chair, but she was wearing her shorts and a T-shirt over her bathing suit now and tapping their room card against her knee.

"Finboy!" his father's voice called out from the pool. Royce looked and saw his father treading water. Wet and slicked back, his hair looked darker, and there was less of it near his forehead than Royce had imagined. It seemed to Royce that grown-ups rarely looked like themselves wet. His mother looked puffy and dazed when she got out of the shower. Royce preferred both of his parents dry.

"In some ways it's the most obvious combination. I'm sure you would've been getting to it next," his father said.

"Who's hungry for lunch?" Royce's mother said, looking only at Royce. Royce waved goodbye to his father and followed his mother to the elevator, which was directly past the vending-machine area. He wished that he had brought a T-shirt to wear. He wrapped the small pool towel around his shoulders and squinted ahead at the video machines, but the boy was gone.

"Don't let him get to you," his mother said as they got on the elevator, tousling Royce's damp hair. "He means well."

Royce felt his eyes shutting and quickly blinked them open. The only time he ever napped anymore was during the in-between week.

"And he's your father," she said, as if Royce didn't already know that.

*

When Royce woke up, he was alone in a double bed in his hotel room. On the bed across from him, he saw a metal tray with a flower laid across it and a note written half in cursive, half in print—his mother's handwriting—next to it. "Mom!" he called out. When no one answered, he decided to struggle through the note. He saw his name at the top and her name at the bottom. He read the words *lunch* and *no french fries* and a sentence that seemed to be the most important one in the paragraph, *Be back soon.*

Royce tried to put the note down on the little table between the beds, but the table was already covered with his and his mother's things: thin neon markers and a new Star Wars coloring book, a half-filled glass of water, jars of vitamins, a hardback library book with the laminated bookmark he made for his mother in kindergarten stuck in the middle of it, half a raisin granola bar. He laid the note down on his mother's bed, put the flower in the half-filled glass of water on the little table and opened the metal cover to check out his lunch: a huge plain hamburger on a bun with seeds in it, potato salad, and a glass of milk in the kind of cup kings drank out of in fairy tales. He leaned over and took a sip of the milk without picking up the glass. He pulled the seeds off the bun and made a little pile out of them on the edge of the plate, then took a bite of his hamburger. It was brown in the middle and tasted okay, but he felt afraid to eat it all alone. "Mom!" he tried again.

She only did this to him at hotels. At home, she never left him. Or at least if she did, Chris was always there when he woke up. Probably she didn't think she'd really left him at all. She treated hotels as if they were big houses, talking to him in the hallways and elevators about his father as if they were all alone, not reminding him to wear a shirt with this bathing suit when they left their hotel room.

Royce was pretty sure his mother was still in the building. He took another bite of his hamburger and imagined her trying to swim laps in the indoor-outdoor pool, wearing her bathing cap and goggles as if she were at the Y back home. Then he remembered the candy machine and the video games and the boy who folded the dollar bill, and he gave up on trying to eat his hamburger and put it down between the potato salad and the little pile of seeds. He planned to feed the seeds to the birds when his mother came back. She'd hold onto his hips while he leaned out the hotel window and called, "Here, birdie, birdie, birdie."

He had to pee, but Royce decided to wait until he got downstairs and then he'd use the bathroom in the lobby near the restaurant where the three of them had dinner the night before. Probably, down there, there would be someone else in the bathroom, either peeing next to him or at least washing his hands in the sink across from him. He hoped no one would be hiding in a stall. Royce put on a shirt and thought about changing his bathing suit but decided not to because it was already dry and because he didn't have to wear underpants under it, and it felt secretive and interesting not wearing any underpants.

Royce thought about propping open the hotel room door with his mother's book so he could get back in, but then he thought about the man who might be hiding in the bathroom stall downstairs and bad men in general and decided to let the door close and lock behind him. In the yellow, buzzing light of the hallway, he thought about how he could have written her a note on the back of her note, but when he tried the door, it was already locked shut, and he knew it was too late for that.

His father's room was across from theirs the way it always was during the in-between week, but he couldn't remember which number it was. He was pretty sure it was room 326 but it could be room 328.

He remembered his father had held his hand up so Royce could high-five him when he said *even* instead of *odd*, but remembering this didn't help because all of the numbers on the other side of the hallway were even. Although he wasn't very good at math for the most part, Royce was nearly expert at even numbers. The only time he had failed to identify one this year was when he was called on in school by a substitute who had thrown him off by using the word *digit*.

Royce thought about his father and trick questions and decided against knocking at the door of room 326 or 328 to tell him he was going to look for his mother. Instead, he followed the signs to the elevator, pushed the down button, and rode to the lobby alone. When the doors opened, he was facing the gift shop. A lady who looked much too old to play with stuffed animals was holding up a tiger and looking at it as if she expected it to start talking to her. "I just don't know," the lady said, although no one besides Royce and the man who worked behind the cash register was there to answer her.

Royce's bladder hurt and he remembered the bathroom around the corner but decided to pee in the pool instead. Although he knew it was an unsanitary thing to do, the image of a man hiding in a bathroom stall had moved into a place in his head and settled in there like a fact. Royce got back on the elevator and pushed the button with the word *Pool* next to it. But when he stepped off, he thought he had made a mistake. The floor felt too dry on his feet, and he didn't hear babies squealing, but the air smelled right, warm and chemical.

He turned and passed the video games and candy machine and walked up the three steps that led to the pool area. At the top, he was stopped by two orange cones and a sign that read *Closed for* something—the last word was too long and Royce couldn't read it. He looked back at the elevator, which looked farther away than it should have, and decided to step around the cones and slide his body quietly into the pool.

He felt the urine leaving him before his chin was even wet and closed his eyes in relief.

"What, can't you read yet?" he heard and looked up to see the nearly teenage boy staring down at him.

Royce shook his head.

"Closed for maintenance. Get your butt out of there."

"You work here?" Royce said.

"My brother's the lifeguard. For two bucks, I patrol the area."

"Cool," Royce said.

"Look, are you going to get out or what?"

Royce swam underwater over to the steps and got out. He had forgotten to take his shirt off and it was wet.

"What's maintenance mean?" Royce asked, looking around for a towel but not finding any.

The boy shrugged. "That's the sign he always puts up when he goes out to his car to smoke weed."

Although Royce didn't know anything about video games, he knew what weed was. Chris smoked it sometimes at night on the back porch with the ceiling fan spinning above him. Once, when Royce couldn't fall asleep, and it was a sleepover night for Chris and his mother was already in bed, Chris let him sit on his lap out there while he smoked. They watched the fireflies light up the yard and neither of them said a word. Sometimes, during Christmas and summer, he missed Chris more than he missed his mother, but he felt bad when this happened.

His father didn't always have the same girlfriend the way his mother had the same boyfriend. "I'm not great on follow-through," his father told Royce once last summer when he was drinking wine after dinner on the balcony of his condominium. Royce was making a domino maze on the floor around his chair and thinking about the wiry dark hair on his father's toes and how he hoped both that this would and would never happen to him. "What do you think? Does your mother ever miss me?" Royce had shrugged so he didn't hurt his father's feelings, but he thought the answer was probably *no*.

*

"You want to see something wild?" the boy said to Royce.

"Okay," Royce said. He followed the boy around to the end of the outside pool to a metal gate that the boy unlatched and opened. Royce looked at the grass and woods and said, "So, where are we going?"

"You'll see," the boy said.

Royce followed the boy into the woods, which smelled damp and flat.

"Okay," the boy said. "This is it." He pointed at the ground.

Royce looked down and saw a trail of four small, dead, featherless birds. They looked like just-hatched baby dinosaurs to Royce. He felt the piece of hamburger settle in his stomach.

"Cool, huh," the boy said. "They must have fallen out of their nest. I know everything about this place," the boy said. "My brother and me live right over there." He pointed through the woods, where Royce could just make out the shape of a road.

Royce knew he was in the state of New Jersey, between his mother's state of Maryland and his father's state of New Hampshire, but he couldn't remember what town they were in this time. His parents took turns picking the towns and hotels for the in-between week, but next year Royce planned to ask if he could pick out a town himself. "I better go back now," Royce said.

"Let me show you something first," the boy said. He stepped behind Royce, and Royce could feel the boy's hands move under his wet shirt and his fingers press in below his ribs. "This is what you do if someone's drowning," the boy said, "and you have to get the water out."

Royce felt the boy's fingers pressing and his body tight against his back, and he stood very still. The boy's breath stopped and then came out in bursts. Royce heard someone splash through the water of the pool and shut his eyes. "Do you think mermaids would ever go in a swimming pool?" Royce asked.

"Christ, you're just a stupid kid," the boy said, pulling his hands and body away.

Royce followed the boy back through the woods toward the hotel. He could see the lifeguard doing the backstroke across the outdoor pool.

"You bet you can kiss your two bucks goodbye this time," the lifeguard said to the boy as they walked past him.

"Up yours," the boy said.

Royce stopped and blinked to adjust his eyes when they walked inside, and when he opened them, the boy was already standing by the video games, sifting through his pocket for quarters. Royce walked past him and pushed the *up* button by the elevator. His bathing suit was almost dry but his shirt was still wet, and he felt the cool air from the air-conditioner next to his skin.

He got off on the third floor and knocked on his door, but his mother still wasn't back. He stared across the hallway at rooms 326 and rooms 328, knocked first at one and then at the other, then stood between the two and waited to see if either would open. The door to room 326 opened, and his mother and father both stood in the door-way. "You just getting up, Finboy?" his father asked.

"Sleepy bird," his mother said and reached out to rub his head.

Royce peered into his father's room. One bed was unmade, and the pillows were missing from the other one.

"Your mother and I were just talking about you, Finboy," his father said.

"Let's get you dressed," his mother said. She gave his father's hand a squeeze and stepped out into the hallway with Royce, slid her room key into their door. "Sometimes grown-ups have a hard time getting things right," she said, and Royce nodded. His mother walked to the bathroom, and Royce saw that her T-shirt was on backwards. Royce thought about Chris sitting on their back porch in Maryland, waiting for his mother to come back. Then he felt the boy's body pressing tight against his back. Royce felt sleepy again, as if he hadn't really napped at all. He climbed back under the covers and listened to the toilet flush, the water run.

Repeat After Me

When Ben gets home from work, Claire is sitting on the living room couch listening to a "French Made Easy" tape, repeating phrases after the speaker, asking for a hotel room that doesn't overlook the street. The speaker is a woman with an encouraging, assured voice. She's the sort of person, Ben thinks, who is certain of getting the room of her choice. Claire's accent is bad, but she is trying and her tone is upbeat, so when she waves at Ben from the couch, he tries too, tells Claire *bonjour* and kisses her lightly on each cheek in a way that he hopes she will perceive as French.

Claire has invited everyone they know who has been to France for dinner tonight. When Ben walks into the kitchen, he sees the ingredients for a vegetable and shrimp casserole spread out on the table. Despite the fact that he is bored with this particular meal (one of Claire's four "company" dishes), Ben is relieved that she is making a predictable recipe and not something difficult and French—a cheese soufflé, for example—that might easily fail her.

Because he read somewhere that vegetables should breathe, Ben loosens the twist-ties on each of the plastic baggies. Then he opens the refrigerator and takes out a beer. Ben can hear Claire in the living room asking for directions. For a moment he forgets what is *left* and what is *right*, but then he falls back on a trick he learned in high school: reversing the alphabetical order of the English words to match them up with their alphabetized companion words in French. This trick isn't particularly complicated, but Ben is disturbed that he has to resort to it. *South* and *north* are easier, but how do you ask where the train station is? Then Ben remembers that he and Claire are planning to rent a car and he feels relieved that he can avoid humiliating himself by stumbling over this one question. Ben has led Claire to believe he is fluent, but it's been years since he's studied French, and he has forgotten very basic things.

It was Claire's idea that they go to France. She thought that it might put the energy back into their marriage. Ben doesn't like Claire using a word like *energy* to describe their marriage (it makes him envision them as baffled cartoon characters, arms outstretched, joined together by a bolt of lightning), but he has to admit that things have changed between them. Mostly, Ben feels, it is Claire who has changed, pulling away from him as if in a constant state of anger.

Claire looks to Ben for an answer because he has been married before and she hasn't, but he doesn't have one to give. His first marriage took place seven years ago and lasted less than a year. It was nothing like his marriage to Claire, which to Ben is a much more substantial thing. "It wasn't the same at all last time," Ben tells her when pressed. "I wasn't expecting that I'd have to compare that with us." This dismissal is never enough for Claire. It leaves her moving around the house, plucking piles of matted dog fur off the furniture, complaining about the mess.

The dogs are fighting with each other on the patio, and Ben opens the back door to yell at them to stop it. Even though he and Claire own this house, Ben worries about being evicted. It is the first house he's ever owned, and while at times he feels proud of it, as if he is somehow personally responsible for the beauty of the irregularly cut, heavy oak floors, the impossible delicacy of the multipaned French windows, more often than not the house worries him—the way the surface of the wood scratches under Claire's heels and the wind blows through the ragged caulk around the thin panes of glass. And, of course, there is the noise and the damage the dogs make, chasing each other throughout the house, the large one wagging his tail against the white walls, leaving paintbrush-like water stains whenever he comes in from the rain.

Each of the dogs is bad in its own way. The little one digs holes in the flower boxes and chews on the roots of Claire's carefully spaced geraniums. The big one is generally friendlier but clumsy. He wags his tail hard against everything and has broken four long-stemmed wine glasses out of a set of eight by knocking them off the coffee table in stupid happiness. Still, Ben cannot imagine his life without the dogs. Each morning before work, together the three of them watch the sun rise in the distance, the dogs disarmingly well-behaved this one time of day, walking unleashed down the slim, exposed medium of Pennsylvania Avenue while cars speed past on either side.

During the first year of Ben and Claire's marriage, Ben brought the small dog home to Claire as a present. Ben and Claire were still renters then, and because their building had a no pet policy, they had to walk the dog late at night and early in the morning so they didn't run into anyone on the elevator. Some mornings they'd meet the paperboy as they got off on the ground floor. They'd hurry past him, the dog sliding on his toenails across the tiled lobby. "It was better when we were renters," Claire says, whenever she is at a loss to explain what is wrong now.

Claire is normally annoyed with the dogs, but tonight when she comes out to the patio and sits next to Ben, she calls them each over to her one at a time and rubs them behind the ears, which causes their jaws to go slack with gratitude. Ben can still hear the woman on the tape in the living room talking although no one is repeating after her anymore. She seems to be ordering a beer, and this seems odd to him because she has the voice of someone who would much prefer wine.

"I don't trust her," he says to Claire.

"You don't trust whom?" Claire says.

"That woman on the tape. That's whom. I don't think she's really a beer drinker."

"The woman on the tape?" Claire says.

"You're still repeating," he says.

"You gave me the damn tape. Why are you drinking already? Please don't do this to me tonight," she says. Then Claire lets up on the dogs, and, as if she has just successfully ordered the beer herself, takes the can from Ben's hand.

*

Although he knows almost everyone at their dinner party, they all seem slightly unfamiliar to Ben tonight, with their expectant, forced smiles. And they seem to be eating too quickly. While they chew mouthfuls of green peppers, they offer advice about what to see in France and how to travel. Ben realizes partway through dinner that Claire is leaning toward purchasing a train pass now, is being convinced that this is a far more economical way to go.

"And you'll meet more people that way," Jackie says, smiling in the way she has that causes her upper gums to show. She has, Ben thinks, an overly robust, camp counselor kind of assurance.

Ben would like to pretend that he doesn't know what his thoughtful, dark wife sees in someone as obvious as Jackie, but he knows Claire too well to do this. He knows that she likes Jackie because she is familiar to Claire, who has a group of friends like her from high school. He met several of them at her ten-year reunion—tall, loud women with large teeth. They send Claire letters with all kinds of messages written on the backs of the envelopes in a private female language that Ben doesn't know how to decode. "What is S.W.A.K.?" he once asked Claire. "Oh, Ben, weren't you ever a teenager?" Claire said.

Although Ben doesn't much like Claire's old friends, he is touched by her loyalty to them, moved in a way that he cannot explain. But while her friendships with her old Jackie-like friends may be endearing to Ben, Claire's friendship with Jackie herself is another matter. Jackie and Claire do not exchange chatty monthly letters from a distance but see each other every day at the office, talk on the phone most nights while Ben reads the paper in the living room and tries not to listen.

When Claire's voice gets quiet, he assumes that she is complaining about their marriage. He's told Claire his suspicion that she's been gossiping about them with people at her office, and she's told him that this is absurd, that she is entitled to her privacy and that she may just have private thoughts that don't have to do with him, did he ever think of that? He has.

For example, he's often wondered what she really thinks of Leonard. Why Leonard, the closest thing Claire has to a first husband, is still hanging around while Ben hasn't seen his own actual first wife in nearly five years. Tonight Leonard is sitting to Ben's right, nodding in agreement with Jackie. Ben doesn't like it that Leonard nods his head in such an unnaturally vigorous way. He likes it even less that after Leonard has finally finished nodding, he begins to make little sucking noises while skimming his tongue back and forth over his front teeth, clearing off food residue that may have settled there, as if he were eating alone.

Holly, the woman sitting across from Leonard, his date, is the only person at their party Ben just met tonight. Although Leonard is tall, his girlfriends are all small and not quite noticeably misshapen, with a slight C-curve in the spine or one leg that is an inch shorter than the other. Some of Leonard's girlfriends wear little-girl pinafore dresses and no makeup at all. Others dress in tight jeans and have spiky hair. This one is of the tight jeans and spiky hair variety. She interrupts the conversation by yawning loudly, and everyone stops talking and looks at her.

"I guess it's time for dessert," Claire says.

Ben gets up and helps her collect the dishes. In the kitchen while she whips cream in the blender, Claire asks him what's wrong. "You don't seem to be having much fun," she says. "I'm starting to think you don't even want to go to France. If you're doing this just for me, don't."

"I do want to go. I just don't see why you always have to invite *him* to every party we have," Ben says. "And," he says, "I wanted to drive. I was kind of counting on that."

"I wish you'd let up on Leonard. You should know by now that he's no threat. Besides I think he's really in love this time."

"Is that what he told you?"

Claire turns off the blender. "No," she says, whispering now. "I just know him, that's all. I can tell by the way he looks at her."

When Ben and Claire bring the dessert into the dining room, Ben looks at Leonard to see what Claire means by this look of love. The problem is that Leonard won't look at his new girlfriend. He's looking instead at a map spread out on the table in front of him and explaining how the subway system works in Paris. "It's exactly like D.C.," he says, and then as if everyone in the room doesn't live in D.C., as if they are all completely unfamiliar with their own subway system, he proceeds to describe the automated method of purchasing tickets in Paris (which *is* exactly the same as the automated method of purchasing tickets in D.C.). Yet no one interrupts Leonard. The only reason Ben doesn't interrupt him himself is because if he does, Claire will let him have it later, telling him that his hostile comments ruined the party she worked so hard at trying to pull off.

Everyone is looking at the map except for Leonard's new girlfriend, who is standing in the corner of the dining room, looking at books on the bookshelf. Daria, who's seven months pregnant, is standing up and leaning across the table with one hand placed on her abdomen, protecting it. Her husband, Eric, is next to her, leaning forward too, tracing his finger down the map and talking about wine country.

Daria and Eric have identically styled, short brown hair. Claire has told Ben that Daria's hair isn't naturally wavy the way Eric's is—it's been permed. Still, Ben is impressed and somewhat saddened by how much the two resemble each other with the sleeves of their loose oxford shirts rolled up to the elbow. He imagines them to have similarly slim hips, drooped shoulders easily weighted with the comfort of their perfect marriage.

"Our honeymoon," Eric says, looking up from the map, "we spent sapped."

Tonight Ben is spending drunk, or trying to anyway. Perhaps he's eaten too much, because the wine he's drinking isn't having the desired effect. He finishes what's left in his glass and walks over to Leonard's new girlfriend. He wonders what her deformity is, but so far she's not giving any clues.

"Who's the history nut?" she says to him.

"Me, I guess," he says. "Do you want to go see our dogs? I need to check on them. They're on the patio and probably doing something wrong just about now."

He walks behind her and watches for defects. Maybe she is perfect. Maybe she is the one. Ben suddenly feels more hopeful than he has in months. It occurs to him that if Leonard is finally happy with someone new, that he and Claire can be happy again. This equation is, of course, too simple, but he feels a sense of temporary relief at having thought of it nonetheless.

Holly picks the biggest piece of outdoor furniture Claire and Ben have, a bentwood rocker, and sits down on it, hugging her knees up to her chest. Ben sits on the stoop across from her. The dogs are sniffing her legs, and the little one jumps up on her lap and licks at her mouth.

"Don't be deceived," Ben says. "It may look like love, but he's only tasting your dinner."

"I know something about dogs. Don't worry," she says. Holly clicks open the little oblong purse she wears around her neck, takes out a cigarette and lights it. "So," she says, exhaling, "how long have you known Leonard?"

"I don't know. About four years, I guess. Ever since I've known Claire. He's my wife's friend, really."

"Ah," Holly says. "I thought maybe you two went to school together or something."

"No," Ben says. "Eric. I went to school with Eric." Ben can hear a Bob Dylan song playing on the stereo inside. It's the live version of "Idiot Wind," which means that Claire has decided against a CD and, instead, put in one of the several party tapes she has made up for this evening. Claire was only a child in the sixties, yet two of the tapes she's made are filled with songs by musicians who, though still recording now, were more popular then. Ben, who is ten years older than Claire, smiles to himself, feeling a kind of false nostalgia, imagining knowing his wife in the sixties as somebody's little sister in Danskin bell-bottoms and plastic, dime-store love beads.

"He's kind of arrogant, don't you think?" Holly says. "Leonard, I mean," she adds when Ben looks confused. She looks at Ben skeptically, and Ben isn't sure if she's determining whether it's all right to continue in this vein, or if she's not certain about the validity of her own statement and wants Ben to argue with her.

"Shit," Ben says because in either case Holly doesn't sound like a woman in love.

Holly takes this in stride, continuing as if she hasn't heard it. "I was just noticing tonight the way he uses the word definitive as if he invented it. The definitive Paris cafe, the definitive renovated castle, the definitive side-trip from Lyon. Puh-leeze," she says.

As if to punctuate her drawn out *please*, Holly exhales a last heavy stream of smoke, and then throws her half-finished cigarette over the fence that separates Ben and Claire's courtyard from their neighbor's, a shadowy man, who, after a year, has not yet introduced himself. Because he can see into the neighbor's courtyard from the bedroom window, Ben knows it is used primarily as a storage area for cans of paint and thinner and other chemical solvents, and after Holly tosses her cigarette, he braces himself for an explosion. When none follows, Ben breathes out audibly as if he's exhaling a stream of cigarette smoke himself.

"I've just met him recently. I go more for the indoor type usually, but Leonard, he's outdoorsy, isn't he? I think he told me he's a hiker or something. Or biker? Not a motorcycle—a bicycle I mean. Is that it? Anyways, he won't let me smoke in his car. Can you stand that? Not even with the window rolled completely down. I told him I nearly quit, that I was down to just two a day now. One in the morning and one after dinner. Can you stand it? I'm lying to a guy I don't even care about. If his timing had been a little bit different, I couldn't see myself with him at all. Not at all. But seeing how the timing was the way it was, here I am." Holly holds the little dog up and looks at it in the eyes. The big dog hates this and starts barking for attention.

Ben holds the big dog between his legs to quiet it. "Timing?" he says.

"Seeing how I just got out of the hospital with this stupid bladder thing. I was feeling vulnerable, like maybe I should meet a nice guy and kind of quiet my life down. What do you think?"

"I don't know much about your life," he says.

"Not that it was sex-related or anything. Don't get me wrong."

"What?"

"The *infection*," Holly says. "It got me thinking though, not while I was in the hospital, but after I got out. For example, yesterday I see this woman on the metro carrying a tray of deviled eggs, not even covered with cellophane, just carrying them out in front of her like she might have been hosting a party instead of walking through rush hour, and I thought, that could be me. I could do that. Forget the cellophane. Do you know what I mean?"

"No. I'm not much of a host myself, though."

"Forget it," Holly says, taking out another cigarette. "Sometimes I get started and there's no stopping me. People who know me better know that about me. 'Put a lid on it, Holly,' is what they always say."

This time she offers Ben a cigarette, and although he doesn't normally smoke, he accepts it because he can see from the odd, oblong shape of the box, a box that fits snugly in Holly's small purse, that the cigarettes seem to be foreign, maybe even French. European, Ben thinks. Now I'm getting in the spirit of things. The cigarette is surprisingly strong, and Ben suppresses a cough as he inhales.

Inside the house Jackson Browne is now singing about wanting to be rocked on the water. While Ben shares Claire's fondness for Dylan and the Stones, he is not fond of Jackson Browne, a whiny, rich, pretty boy who acts as if he has known nothing but suffering. Hearing Jackson Browne sing makes Ben feel generally annoyed and then, gradually, more specifically annoyed with Holly for not being in love with Leonard, for not marrying him and taking him out of his wife's life.

The door behind Ben opens and Eric sits down on the stoop next to him. "Smoke?" he says, holding out an unlit joint.

Holly shakes her head. "I can't. I'm on medication. Actually my doctor didn't say anything about smoking pot exactly, but I'm not supposed to drink. Ginger ale," she says, pointing at the glass by her chair. "So I guess I'm not supposed to smoke either. Pot, that is. Can you imagine asking your doctor if it's okay to smoke pot?"

"I don't know," Eric says, twisting one end of the joint. "When I was a teenager, I had asthma for a while, and this one doctor I went to, he told me to inhale on the inhaler—that's what the asthma medicine's kept in—the same way I'd inhale a joint. Then he demonstrated for me how to do this. With the inhaler. He just pretended to inhale it. The cap was still on and everything. He sure looked like he was smoking a doobie, though, his lips all puffed out and everything. My mother was right there, too, sitting in this guy's office in the seat next to me. I had to play real dumb, like I had no idea what this guy was talking about." Eric lights the joint and passes it to Ben.

"What? Did you grow up in California or something?" Holly asks.

"No, New Jersey."

The pot is having a little more of an effect on him than the wine has had, but Ben still feels sadly sober. He stares up over Holly's head to the sky to see what kind of moon it is.

"Good dinner, Ben. Good party," Eric says. Eric puts his arm around Ben's back and slaps him lightly before pulling his arm away.

Since he's been married, Eric's become the most affectionate guy that Ben knows. Even if he's just coming by to borrow the hedge trimmers, he hugs Ben goodbye. Whenever Eric and Daria walk by Ben and Claire's house, they're holding hands. Before he met Daria, Eric wasn't this way, or at least that's not the way Ben remembers him. Eric used to live down the hall from Ben back in college. They weren't good friends then, but still it had been a surprise for them both to discover each other living on the same block in the same city thirteen years later.

Ben remembers dropping acid one night with Eric back in college and going out to a neighborhood bar. Eric picked up two local high school girls and brought them back to their dorm. At first Ben figured that one of the girls was supposed to be for him, but Eric brought both into his dorm room and shut the door behind him. Ben stood for a while outside his door listening, the fluorescent lights in the hallway singing above him, then finally walked down the hall to his room and went to sleep.

"I heard they give it to people with emphysema sometimes," Holly says.

"What?" Eric says.

"Marijuana. For the pain."

"Oh right," Eric says. He offers a last hit to Ben, then stubs it out between his thumb and index finger. Eric takes a 5th Avenue bar out of his pocket, and, before Ben can stop him, throws the wrapper over the fence into the neighbor's courtyard. Doesn't anyone realize that this courtyard belongs to someone?

"Well," Eric says, "I'd better go see about Daria. I get nervous if I leave her alone too long."

"When is she due?" Holly asks.

"Not for another two months, but you can't ever tell for sure. Sometimes she gets these contraction-like pains. Once we even made a trip to the emergency room, but it turned out to be a false alarm. Braxton-Hicks they're called, to be specific."

"Wow," Holly says. "No one's ever loved me that much."

Ben worries that Eric is going to walk over to Holly and lean down and hug her, tell her that he loves her.

But Eric doesn't hug Holly. Instead he sighs deeply, then smiles, stands up and walks back inside the house, where Mick Jagger is singing about every girl who has ever taken anything from him. Most women find this song sexist and intolerable, but not Claire. At this moment Ben loves this about Claire.

Ben wants to completely clear up this thing about Leonard and

Holly before going back inside. "No way are you going to marry Leonard, right?" he says.

"Marry him? Did he say that?"

"No. It was just a stupid idea I came up with from the way he looked at you. You know, like it was love."

"Well, you're way off-base here. Marry him. Jesus."

"Okay. Well, I should probably head back inside now, do my host bit."

"Go ahead. I'll just sit out here for a while."

When Ben gets back inside, he finds Claire by herself in the kitchen, rinsing plates out in the sink. Her hair is hanging over her cheeks, and she looks very young. He is filled with happiness at their luck, that she doesn't have asthma, that there is nothing wrong with her bladder. He sucks lightly on the back of her neck, and she pulls away from him.

"You smell like a wine factory," Claire says.

"I don't think that's what they're called, wine factories," he says. "Anyway, she's not the one. Her bladder. There's something wrong with it."

"Jesus, does everything have to be perfect with you?"

"I'm just saying that you're wrong about her being the one. I don't think she is."

He leaves Claire with her good health and anger in the kitchen and walks into the living room where the party has moved. Leonard is leaning on the window ledge, where he can monitor the entire room while turning his head a nearly imperceptible amount. Ben cringes, thinking about how fragile the wood is on which Leonard is supporting his weight.

Eric is giving Jackie a foot rub on the couch. She is leaning back against an arm of the couch, and her feet, which are surprisingly small and nicely shaped, are placed in Eric's lap.

Daria is smiling, sitting cross-legged by the fireplace skimming through a notebook that is opened on top of her belly, which she appears to be using as a kind of table. Claire's third party tape, the one with newer music on it, is playing now. Ben doesn't know what group this is. All of the new music Claire listens to sounds similar to him, a little too earnest and heartfelt, as if Jackson Browne's offspring are writing and performing it.

"Ben, we were just beginning to wonder where you had gone off to," Daria says, looking up. "I know this probably seems silly, but when Claire told me that this party was about your trip, I thought it might be fun to bring my journal from the first time I was in France, before Eric. I was just telling Jackie that I wrote down everything. You know how it is when you're young."

He suspects that Claire suggested to Daria that she bring her journal. It is the sort of ploy his wife would come up with, Ben thinks, neither kindly nor critically. "Well, read," he says because he doesn't see any way of getting out of this. "Let's hear it."

He turns down the volume on the stereo, and Daria opens to the middle of her journal and begins reading about her train trip from Paris to Aix. Despite the fact that she has described the countryside in detail, Ben can see nothing particularly France-like about any of it. If the people around her weren't all speaking French, she could have been riding a train up to Massachusetts from New York.

When she gets to Aix, the date changes on her entry, skips ahead two days, and then she reads about the hotel where she is staying. "'Every morning I go downstairs at eight and have my coffee and a roll with the other guests in the dining room. Most of the guests are foreigners, too, except for one, Philippe, who is from Dijon,'" Daria reads. "I better stop here," Daria says. "It begins to get a little personal if I remember correctly. Why don't I just skip ahead to Carcassonne? You guys have to go there. Promise me you won't skip Carcassonne."

"Oh, come on," Jackie says, smiling her gummy smile. "Keep reading. I bet this is where it gets good."

Eric stops rubbing her feet, and Jackie bends her knees and tucks them back under her.

"Okay," Daria says, fluffing out her bangs with her fingers the way she might if she had just woken up. "A little more maybe. I mean we're all adults here, right? And this was a *long* time ago."

She reads about how Philippe says that he'll show her around town, and how soon they begin to fall in love. "Not real love," she adds quickly, looking up at Eric, who is up from the couch now and has begun pacing around the room. "Just puppy stuff."

"'Philippe,'" Daria reads, "'has dark hair and small, brown, hairless nipples. Tonight he made love to me by the sea, pushing my shoulders and the blade of my spine into the sand.'"

Jackie giggles and Ben looks across the room at Leonard, who is leaning back against the window with a small, knowing smile as if Daria is reading about the beauty of *his* nipples.

"Jesus," Daria says. "I must have been reading romances. Uh-oh, I really better stop here," she says, looking at Eric.

"Why stop there? Why stop now?" Eric says, still pacing. Ben's never seen Eric like this before, or at least he hasn't seen him look like this in years. Eric has the same nervous, wired-up look that he had when the two of them dropped acid and went to that neighborhood bar, when he told two girls that they wouldn't be sorry if they came back with him.

Ben can't believe that Claire is missing this, the one fight that they will probably ever be able to witness between Daria and Eric, the couple Claire compares them with unfavorably when she complains about their own marriage. He backs up out of the living room and goes into the kitchen to find her, so they can experience this moment of imperfection in other peoples' lives together, but she's not there. He opens the back door and finds her leaning forward on the stoop in the courtyard, talking in a low voice to Holly.

"You're missing it," he says. "A fight in the living room."

"A fight?" she says, standing up.

"Well, not a fist fight or anything. A verbal fight. Tensions mounting. Blood pressure rising."

"Shit, Ben," Claire says, sitting back down. "Can't you see we're talking? You're the host. Why don't you break it up? Change the subject or something. And put on some music. What happened to my tape?"

Holly tosses her cigarette butt into the neighbor's courtyard and glares at Ben as if he is the kind of man who normally enjoys fights, as if perhaps he even causes them just so he can relish them. He is certain that she glares. This is more than he can take. A woman he hardly knows glaring at him in his own house.

He goes back inside and sits by himself at the dining room table with the map of France spread out in front of him and finishes up the wine straight from the bottle, the way they drink in France, he'll tell Claire if she catches him at this. He can hear that Daria has stopped reading now, has probably put her journal safely back in her purse where it belongs.

When Ben hears the doorbell ring followed by the dogs barking, for a moment he feels confused by the sounds, shifts through the list of possible disturbing noises—alarm clock, telephone, fax machine—before identifying it. He has been asleep for the past few minutes at the dining room table, the side of his face resting against the soft sheen of the map. "I'll get it!" he finally yells a little too loudly. But when he enters the living room, Leonard has already opened the door.

Leonard steps to the side and a man who looks familiar to Ben, but whom he cannot quite place, walks in the front door. His belly protrudes a little too much over his belt buckle for him to be one of the joggers who passes him on the median each morning as he walks the dogs. Still, he looks familiar to Ben in the same blurred way these joggers look as they pass by without nodding.

Ben takes a step closer, extends his hand and introduces himself. "What can I help you with?" he says.

"You're the owner, aren't you?" the man says. "I'm your neighbor, Richard Mahoney. My friends call me Rich. You can call me Richard."

Ben laughs, assuming that Richard Mahoney is making a rather feeble joke, but when he doesn't smile back at him, Ben stops laughing and remembers all of the debris that has been tossed all night long into the courtyard next door. "Oh, you're the man on *that* side," Ben says.

"I don't know what you mean by *that* side, but if you mean the side you and your friends have been using as a fucking garbage can all night long, that's the side I'm on."

Ben wants to tell Richard Mahoney that he hasn't been the one who's been tossing the garbage, that he has, in fact, silently objected to this behavior, but there wouldn't be any point in protesting now that the damage has already been done. Besides, Ben suddenly is feeling defensive—this is his home, these people in his house, even the offenders, are his friends. If this man has a problem, they will deal with it man to man, no harm done, no reason for anyone to talk so rudely.

Just as Ben is getting ready to calmly paraphrase his thoughts, Eric steps up next to him and says, "Listen, man, watch your mouth. There are women present here, and there's no need for you to talk that way."

"Sweetheart," Daria says, pushing herself up from the hearth of the fireplace. "Why don't you let Ben handle this? It's his house, after all."

"Why don't you let Ben handle this?" the neighbor mocks in a singsong voice.

Daria pulls on Eric's shirt to keep him from stepping forward.

"I'll tell you what," Richard says, "I'm not usually so diplomatic, but tonight I don't care which one of you boys handles this, as long as that fucking garbage gets picked up out of my backyard." Richard walks out the front door without pulling it shut behind him. The dogs, who had been watching him from a safe distance, walk up to the entranceway now and sniff at the section of floor where Richard Mahoney had stood. For a moment no one moves to shut the door, then Ben finally pushes it closed.

"How do you like that," Claire says, standing in the doorway to the living room with Holly. "We finally meet the mystery neighbor. I guess he forgot to bring a welcome cake with him. Honey," she says to Ben, "you should have offered him something to drink."

Ben feels startled, as if perhaps he is truly being chastised for being a bad host, but Daria and Jackie both laugh, and he is relieved to find that his wife is kidding. He cannot quite bring himself to laugh, but he forces a smile in Claire's direction to show her that he is grateful that she is trying to lighten things up.

"Damn," Leonard says, sitting down on the couch next to Jackie.

"What that guy needs are some real problems to worry about. Just think how far he could go toward solving, say, world hunger if he channeled some of that anger."

"Well," Claire says, "you have a good point, but for some reason I don't quite see this happening."

Ben watches as Claire and Leonard exchange small, private-looking smiles. Is he only imagining that their smiles refer to some secret joke between them? A joke about channeling maybe? This is something that Claire has made fun of to him before, this whole idea of channeling, the dead choosing to speak through otherwise unexceptional middle-aged women. Do Claire and Leonard giggle about this same thing, or has Ben missed the meaning of their exchange completely? In his peripheral vision, Ben can see Holly fidgeting, rocking slightly forward and then back onto her heels in a grating rhythm.

"I threw one damn candy wrapper over the fence," Eric says. "And I didn't know I was throwing it into some bozo's yard, believe me. If he could walk all the way over here, he could just as well walk out his own back door and pick it up himself."

"That doesn't seem to be the point," Daria says.

For some reason Ben feels like imitating Daria's voice the way Richard Mahoney did. *That doesn't seem to be the point.* Instead, he says, "I'll go. Everyone just relax. This doesn't have to be a big problem."

"I don't know," Claire says, "about you going over there by yourself, I mean. What do we know about this guy, after all? We've lived here for a nearly a year, and he's never introduced himself up until tonight. And then he's got such an attitude about him. Maybe I should go with you."

"Yeah, right," Ben says. "I'm going to let my wife walk into some possibly schizoid guy's house with me." Ben feels a hint of a chill pass up through his backbone. For the first time since he's known her, he's almost called Claire "my woman" instead of "my wife."

"I'll go over with you," Eric says. "It was my 'fucking' candy bar wrapper."

Ben sees Holly rocking from side to side on her heels now, probably digging wedges inches deep in the floorboards.

"What are we talking about here anyway?" Claire says. "A few cigarette butts, a candy bar wrapper? B.F.D."

Ben imagines one of Claire's girlfriends writing this across the back of an envelope in swirls of purple ink: B.F.D., T.G.I.F., S.W.A.K. He notices that Holly has stopped rocking, as if she is relieved to be caught both at smoking and at littering. For a moment he imagines holding Holly up and lifting her over the fence to pick up the candy wrapper and her half-finished cigarettes. He could hang her from her ankles, and she could hover just above the ground until she found them all, her tiny, doll-like arms stretched down, her spandex top finally succumbing to the pull of gravity, loosening and bunching like layers of baby fat under her arms.

"Listen," Leonard says, interrupting Ben's fantasy, "how about if all the men go over there and just get this thing over with?"

"I really don't see why I can't just go by myself," Ben says.

"Ben," Daria says, "you don't know anything about this guy. Maybe he's a real nut. I mean, who knows? Leonard's got a good idea, I think. Why don't all of the men go over there together and pick up the litter and just get this thing over with?"

And just get this thing over with. "Fine," Ben says, feeling as if there's no way of winning this argument.

The walk next door doesn't leave time for Ben to figure out how he should handle things once they get there, so he knocks on Richard Mahoney's front door and hopes he will know what to say when it's opened. But Richard Mahoney doesn't give him a chance to speak. "Well, I see all you boys decided to be good scouts and clear up this little problem together. That's just fine," he says, signaling them inside.

Ben has no idea how to stop this guy from patronizing him in front of Leonard and Eric. "We'll just head right out back," he says. "Come on, guys. This should only take a few minutes."

Ben is dismayed to see that, although it's furnished differently and seems somewhat messier, the layout of Richard Mahoney's house is exactly the same as that of his own house: living room, dining room, powder room, kitchen, courtyard. Although Ben and Claire looked at enough houses before they purchased their own for Ben to know that this layout is hardly an unusual one in an old row house, he feels saddened to be walking through his own home's mirror image.

"What a dump," Eric says when they get out to the courtyard. "I guess that must give you some idea of what your place might look like if Claire decided to let it go."

"What are you talking about?" Ben says.

"The mess. That guy's a first-class slob is what I'm saying. And it's no better out here. What is all this shit anyway?"

Ben looks around the courtyard at the cans of paint, thinner, and turpentine, the trays and rollers that he already knew would be there, piled haphazardly around the small area. On top of a folding chair, heavy paintbrushes soak in a bucket full of some liquid that looks to Ben as if it may be rainwater. "Exhibit A," he says reaching in and taking out the candy bar wrapper that lay floating in the bucket.

"What about all these cigarette butts?" Leonard says, bending down and picking one up. "Are we supposed to pick them up, too? How do we know they're not the asshole's?"

"Because the asshole doesn't smoke," Richard Mahoney says, pushing the back door open. He points at his open kitchen window, indicating how he could hear this. "It's that little, spooky girl. I saw her throwing them from upstairs. Lit and everything. Just tossing them away over the fence. It was almost pretty. Like they might have been fireflies."

"Yeah, right," Leonard says, picking up a butt, and looking at it in mock amazement, as if he'd never seen one quite like it before. "Beautiful, just beautiful. Give me a break."

"When they were flying through the air, they were pretty. Not now. What do you think I wanted you scouts to clean them up for?" Richard clears a large space off for himself on the stoop and sits down with his feet spaced what seems, to Ben, an unnecessary distance, possibly even a menacing distance, apart. "Hey, I apologize to you boys if I overreacted a little while ago, but I've got an excitable nature. Especially when it comes to my house. A wise man once said a mouthful when he said a man's place is his castle. Nice night, huh? Good night for a party. Not too hot, not too cold."

Ben hears the back door to his house open, but the fence between the two courtyards is too high for him to see over. Ben looks up at Richard, who, from his perch on the stoop, cranes his neck, peering down into Claire and Ben's courtyard. "It was the looker," he says after the door shuts. "She was just bringing some dip or something inside."

Ben thinks two things—he better not be talking about Claire that way, and I hope that it's Claire that he's talking about.

"The looker?" Leonard says.

Ben watches Leonard. Does he hope that Richard Mahoney is talking about Claire, too?

"The blond babe. Which one of you guys is with her anyway?"

"Man, this is none of your business, any of it," Eric says.

"Well, I know she's not your woman," Richard Mahoney says. "You're with the pregnant one. I may not be Einstein, but I've got that much figured out."

"Okay, I think we've got it all. Ready, guys?" Ben says.

"I don't know if we're ready or not," Leonard says. "Perhaps Richard isn't quite through insulting us yet. Are you, Rich? Are you quite through insulting us or have you still got a ways to go? How about our mothers? You haven't started in on them yet."

Ben feels his stomach lurch slightly. He thought it would be Eric, but now it looks as if it's Leonard he has to worry about.

"Hey," Richard says, shrugging his shoulders, "take it easy, guy. Is the pregnant one your wife or something? What did I do, get it all mixed up? As far as I'm concerned maybe you guys all share the women. Maybe you have your own little commune or something. What's it to me? I'll tell you what it is to me. Nothing. That's what it is. Live and let live. That's my motto. Nope, it's nothing at all to me what you boys and girls do until your stuff starts flying over into my courtyard."

"Well that seems fair enough," Ben says.

"Tell you boys what," Richard says. "Just to show you that there's no hard feelings between us now that you've got your litter all cleaned up, why don't you come on inside and have a drink before you head back to your party. In fact, I insist upon it, I insist upon giving you boys a drink on the house."

Ben doesn't know how it happens that none of them refuse this offer. Maybe it's because they're all thinking what Ben's thinking—that there will be no way to make a dignified exit without sitting down with Richard Mahoney for a drink first, pretending somehow that a drink, not picking up cigarette butts, is what they'd originally come here for.

When Ben stands up to walk inside the house, he is dizzy for a moment, caught off-balance from having bent down to pick up the last cigarette butt. The kitchen smells of paint and putty and of a third odor that Ben at first has trouble identifying, but finally decides is air freshener filtering into the kitchen from the bathroom.

Richard says to pardon the mess, that he's in the process of remodeling, and clears off chairs for them at the kitchen table. "Yep, I'm putting all new appliances in here. All that you see here right now is obsolete as far as I'm concerned. It's already out of here. Even this floor your feet are resting upon has already been replaced in my mind. I've got a new one picked out. Quarry tile, not this crummy linoleum."

Ben looks down at the floor. It doesn't look so bad to him. He tries unsuccessfully to remember what his own kitchen floor looks like.

"I see what you mean, buddy," Eric says. "This is real cheap stuff."

"It's not so much that it's cheap as that it's worn down. That's what I meant," Richard says.

"Hey, man, nothing personal," Eric says. "I'm simply agreeing with you that your floor is a piece of shit."

Ben feels his stomach lurch for the second time since they've been here. Through the common brick wall between the two row houses, he can just make out the quick eruption of television laughter. Ben is reassured by the sound and by the image it necessitates for him: four women cleaning up in the kitchen with the television on in the background. He imagines that all women relax, become in some crucial way their better selves, as soon as men leave them alone.

"Okay, have it your way," Richard Mahoney says. "It's a piece of shit, this floor. We're even now, okay? I insult your wife, you insult my floor. She is your wife, the pregnant one? I knew it. I've seen you with her before. Walking past. I guess we'd be even more even if you insulted my wife, too, but seeing as I don't have a wife, or I should say, no longer have a wife, insulting my floor will have to suffice. We'll just call it the next best thing."

"That seems fair," Ben says.

Richard opens a cabinet and takes out a bottle of scotch. Ben notices a discreet white ant trap in the cabinet, although there don't seem to be any ants, and there is clearly no food for the ants to eat. "Rocks or without?" Richard Mahoney says, shutting the cabinet door.

Ben hears the phone ring next door in his kitchen and is surprised at how clear it sounds. He'd always assumed that the brick wall between their houses completely buffered the noises he and Claire made from their neighbor. Although Ben cannot remember hearing Richard Mahoney's phone ring before from his own house, now that he thinks about it, Ben remembers being surprised at hearing the stark hum of Richard's clothes dryer through the basement wall. Are old bricks less effective somehow?

Ben remembers now how when Jackie had said that the bricks needed to be repointed he had hardly listened. Maybe that's the problem. The pointing. He thinks about asking Richard about this repointing business, something he might know about, but decides not to indebt himself by accepting whatever information Richard may have to give.

"Late for a phone call, isn't it?" Richard says. "Nearly midnight."

Ben shrugs. "It's probably just a wrong number."

Realizing now that Richard Mahoney has most certainly heard whole sections of their arguments—Claire's voice rising to a high pitch, his own voice becoming dark and frightening even to him—excerpts from their marriage, Ben feels himself hunch down as if to protect himself from further exposure.

"I notice you get quite a few of those. Late-night calls. More wrong numbers, I imagine," Richard says. "You might think about getting your number changed."

"Jesus, what do you do, sit here and wait for their phone to ring?" Leonard asks. But this time Leonard's voice seems different to Ben, not exactly friendly but impressed. Ben realizes that Leonard has made a decision about Richard and is now treating him like an eccentric instead of an antagonist. He has seen Leonard make this same decision about other people before. While Ben is relieved that at least Leonard and Richard won't be fighting, he is annoyed that this generally unpleasant situation has become a kind of opportunity, an unexpected gift for Leonard.

"I'm going to add a little more water to this," Eric says, standing up, taking his glass over to the sink, and dripping water into it thoughtfully. "You know, Rich has a point. You might think about getting your number changed. Throw the creep off base. Send him on his way. Shit, if it were Daria home alone getting some obscene calls, I couldn't stand it, what for worrying about her."

"They're not obscene. Just hang ups," Ben says.

"Are they breathers?" Richard asks.

"No. I told you, they're not obscene. Just silence and then someone hangs up."

"No heavy breathing at all, is there?" Richard says. "Not even real soft like this?" Richard makes little puffs at the air. "My ex-wife used to get those. Poof, poof, poof, and then a hang up."

"You're too much, man," Leonard says.

"I told you. They're not obscene. Just silence and then a click."

"Of course if they're not breathers, there's always another possibility," Richard says. "But if you haven't already raised it to yourself, I don't need to be the one to raise it for you."

Ben finishes his scotch and pours more into his glass, stirs it around with a partially melted ice cube. He knows what Richard is getting at. It's not like the thought hasn't crossed his mind before. He even read an article in a women's magazine in the dentist's office that highlighted the warning signs of an unfaithful spouse. It made him feel simultaneously more foolish and anxious about his own suspicions. "This particular discussion has now ended," Ben says.

"Hey, no sweat," Richard says. "I thought we were all friends here now, that's all, *mano y mano* and all that good stuff. I'm just speaking from experience, having been married already and all, just trying to share whatever my experience might be able to offer to a younger guy like you, that's all."

"Well, I appreciate that," Ben says. "No harm intended. We'll just let that subject drop."

"No problem. Like I said. I was just trying to be brotherly."

"Too much," Leonard says.

Ben, who considers himself essentially a private person, has never felt his personal life become public so quickly before. He looks down at his drink, wondering who to blame, knowing that if he looks at Leonard, Leonard will be smiling in the small, knowing way he has that makes Ben feel crazy.

"What are you smiling about?" he says, looking up, even though he doesn't intend to. "You're pretty happy, aren't you, to see things all screwed up between Claire and me? I bet you're willing to trade in all your little deformed girlfriends for someone like Claire, aren't you?"

"You're with the little, spooky girl? Shit, that blows me away. I wouldn't have guessed at that combination. I figured you to be with the blond. I guess you never can tell. But, hey, that's my motto," Richard says. "Live and let live."

"Take it easy, Ben," Eric says. He walks over to Ben, stands behind him and massages his shoulders. "Just let all this anger flow out of you. Leonard and Claire were a long time ago. There's nothing happening there now, is there, Leonard? Claire's your wife. You guys are going to France together. It's going to be just like a second honeymoon. Leonard, tell Ben that there's nothing happening between you and Claire."

Eric's fingers feel rubbery and wet through the shoulders of Ben's shirt. Through the wall he hears a quick, high-pitched giggle that he doesn't recognize. Holly. That would be the way Holly would laugh.

"France," Richard says. "Hell, that'll be something special all right. Old Paree is bound to put the romance back in the marriage."

"Tell him, Leonard," Eric says. "Tell him there's nothing to worry about."

Leonard looks at Eric and then down at Ben. "This is absurd. I don't have to tell him anything."

"See, he thinks it's absurd," Eric says, still kneading Ben's shoulders. "May as well be the same thing as saying outright that nothing's going on. Besides Leonard can't be making the phone calls, can he? He's right here with us."

Ben looks at Leonard, who still wears that smug, compact smile on his face that tells him nothing.

Then he looks at Richard Mahoney who is, Ben realizes, despite his slightly protruding belly and the couple of days of growth on his face, the best looking of the four of them, the only one of them that Claire and Jackie might call *macho* with faked disgust. "You know something about women, do you?" Ben says.

"I guess I know a few things."

"And you think my wife's cheating on me?"

"Now, I didn't say that. I just said that it's mighty peculiar to get so many late-night phone calls. I just know that it would be something I'd look into if I was you."

Ben shrugs Eric's fingers off his shoulders.

"Look," Leonard finally says, "I was just trying to get you riled up. There's nothing between Claire and me anymore. Not that I wouldn't like there to be sometimes. I miss her, okay? But she won't have anything to do with me that way. Not since she's been with you. I haven't even tried anything for years. Not since you guys got married, made it official."

"Is this supposed to make me feel better?" Ben says.

"Hey, it's not supposed to make you feel anything. Take it any way you want to. I'm just trying to be honest with you."

"Good man," Eric says. "See, Leonard's not up to anything."

"Boys, boys, boys," Richard says, standing up suddenly. "This conversation has taken an unnecessarily ugly turn. Come on, I'm going to show you something that's going to take your minds off all this."

Ben trails behind as they follow Richard Mahoney out of the

kitchen. He can hear nothing through the wall now, not even the comforting sound of the television.

"Because you were such good scouts about cleaning up your mess, I'm about to let you in on one of my most closely guarded secrets."

Although he suspects he should be frightened, Ben doesn't feel that way as he follows Leonard down the familiar narrow staircase to Richard's basement. Instead, he feels himself succumb slowly to the numbing inevitability of this evening, the inescapableness of whatever is about to happen next.

"Okay, in a minute I'm going to count to three and turn on the overhead light," Richard says when they are all in the basement. "Now you all shut your eyes, so I know for sure none of you boys can see until I've got everything all set up just right."

Ben, who has had trouble adjusting his eyes to the dim light, gladly obeys. He feels as if he is being allowed a small nap, standing there with his eyes closed. Next to him, he can hear Leonard, who he knows is allergic to molds, sniffing in and out loudly, probably anticipating that his sinuses will clog in the stuffy basement air. Ben wonders if he is peeking. Yes, he thinks, probably so. Probably Leonard and Eric are both cheating.

"Okay, almost ready. At the count of three. One, two, three." From across the room Richard Mahoney flips on the bright overhead lights.

Ben hesitates before opening his eyes. When he finally opens them, he feels as disoriented as if he's just walked into an overlit convenience store after having driven through the quiet streets in the darkness of his car. Richard Mahoney is standing like a matador with a white sheet spread out by his hips. His smile becomes more hesitant as his gaze shifts from Eric to Leonard to Ben. "Well, are you going to leave me hanging here all night or is somebody going to say something?"

"Damn," Ben hears Eric whisper.

In the center of the basement, next to Richard Mahoney, stands a wobbly replica of the houses on Ben and Richard's street, nearly as tall as Richard himself, made out of flattened cereal and tampon boxes with cotton swab chimneys.

Leonard and Eric walk over to the sagging miniature rowhouses. Eric taps the pads of his fingers on a courtyard fence built out of what appear to be used Stimudents. Ben takes a step forward and peers through a hole cut into a Tampax box into his own kitchen. Leaning against an empty thread spool is a small, Mexican-looking rag doll, her brown yarn hair hanging down over her cheeks.

"I can't believe you did all this," Eric says, discovering his own house now by counting down aloud.

Richard Mahoney stands back and smiles proudly, surveying his work.

"Too much," Leonard says, staring into a window cut out of a Cocoa Krispies box. "Hey, look. That must be Daria."

Ben and Eric stand next to Leonard and look in at an open-mouthed baby doll, too large for the room already, who has what seems to be nearly an entire roll of toilet paper wrapped around her belly.

"I don't know if I like this," Eric says. "It just makes me wonder."

Richard shrugs. "What's there to wonder about? It's my hobby," he says, reaching in the baby's room and gently patting the doll's stomach. "Pretty clever, huh? Shit, every man's got to have a hobby, doesn't he?"

Ben doesn't have a hobby, but he doesn't say anything. He's too exhausted to argue. Peering into his master bedroom, Ben sees a naked Ken doll lying on his back on a Froot Loops-box floor, one hand placed under his head, the other resting on the inside of his thigh in a way that may or may not be obscene.

Ben hears Jackie shouting: "Hello? Yoo hoo? Anyone here?" and for a minute he's confused about where the sound is coming from. Through the wall of the basement?

"Hey, Jack, we're down here," Leonard shouts. "Come on down. You've got to see this."

It's just like Leonard, Ben thinks, to call Jackie *Jack* in front of Richard Mahoney, who had them erroneously paired up together, as if to insinuate with this absurd diminutive of her already foreshortened name that they are closer than they are.

"What are you guys doing down here, anyway?" she says as she comes down the stairs. "We were starting to get worried, you know. You might have called. Wow," she says when she spots the row of houses.

"Ah, it's nothing," Richard Mahoney says. "Just big dollhouses, really."

In the master bedroom of the replica of Ben's house, Ken-Ben is still lying on the floor with his hand in the position that may or may not be obscene. When Ben reaches in the window to move that hand, to place it perhaps behind his head with his other hand, in a position much less ambiguous in intention, Richard Mahoney grabs his wrist. "Hey, Buddy, what are you doing there? Rule number one. No one rearranges my dolls but me."

Ben quickly moves the hand to the side of the doll before stepping away and watching Richard shrug his shoulders in Jackie's general direction. "Artistic temperament," he smiles.

Her smile back at him is strained, but, still, there it is.

Richard Mahoney makes a great show of carefully covering the houses back up before walking them up to the front door. Ben hears him whisper something to Jackie when they reach the top of the landing. Then Jackie glances at Ben and covers her mouth and giggles.

*

A little while later, back at his own house, Ben will think about this glance, this giggle, about what they might mean. But he won't ask Jackie. He would rather not look at any of them. Originally intending to dust the dining room table, Ben sits at that table instead with the bottle of furniture polish in front of him, in his own house, his guests still there, everyone but Claire in the living room now, retelling the story of Richard Mahoney, Leonard and Eric rushing in to fill in gaps in each other's stories, Jackie's voice rising up to an excited pitch above theirs at irregular intervals.

*

When they first returned from next door, Ben went back to the kitchen to finish the dishes, and Claire came in and asked him what was wrong.

"I know all about it," he said, not looking up, although he was only testing a theory, and of course didn't know anything.

"Know?" Claire asked.

Still staring down at the dishes, Ben nodded his head.

"Oh, Jesus, what did Leonard tell you?" Claire asked.

Ben looked up at her, and Claire stared back. "He didn't say anything, did he?"

Ben shook his head. He felt sorry for his wife, watching her being put on the spot this way, the way her breath quickened as she tucked a stray piece of hair behind an ear.

"Well, that's because there's nothing to say," she said.

"Shh," Ben said, putting his finger up to her lips to keep her from talking.

*

Ben can hear that Claire has finished washing and is drying the last of the dishes in the kitchen. And although it is now quiet enough and he is close enough to make out the entire conversation in the living room, he continues to hear only isolated words and phrases. *Crazy as they make them*, he hears. *Just big dollhouses. Really.*

While Ben was next door, Claire had locked the dogs in the spare bedroom upstairs for the night, and now Ben can hear the little one, still awake, scurrying back and forth above him, chasing after a tennis ball.

The conversation seems to end just as suddenly as it began, as if someone had simply opened up the front door and let the last rushes of words blow back out into the night. After a brief silence, Jackie begins to plan something. Ben can hear her noisily arranging the guests, telling them to stand in certain places. Then, except for the noise above, the house is quiet again.

When he walks into the living room, Ben sees Daria held up in the air, balanced only on index fingers, her pregnant belly a small, strong mound pointed toward the ceiling. Her bare feet are poised on Leonard's fingers, and Eric is delicately balancing her shoulders. Holly and Jackie face each other over her belly, Holly's face twisted into seriousness with whatever words or image Jackie has given her to concentrate on, Ben imagines. Ben catches Leonard's eye, and Leonard winks at him.

The house is disturbingly quiet to Ben. Next door, Richard Mahoney makes no noises. Ben imagines him leaning the side of his head up against their adjoining wall, listening for evidence. Even the little dog seems to have given up for the night. Ben turns from Daria and walks over to his stereo to pick out a tape.

"Oh, play the French one," Jackie says, still balancing a section of Daria. "That's from Dijon. Folk music. I brought it for tonight."

"Fine," Ben says. He doesn't care. Any kind of noise will be fine. As soon as he puts the tape in he realizes that he's made a mistake. Instead of Jackie's tape, Claire's French lesson comes booming out of the speakers. Everyone thinks Ben's mistake is very funny. Even Daria, lifted up above them all, begins to giggle.

Ben doesn't think it's funny, but he doesn't change the tape. He's looking at Leonard and looking at Leonard is all that Ben can do for now. He's still looking at Leonard when Claire walks up, smelling of lemon dish soap. She puts her arms around Ben's waist and whispers in his ear, trying to make up now, so that when everyone leaves and they are alone again their marriage will seem like a substantial thing. She whispers *repeat after me* in suddenly perfect French.

But Ben tells her *no,* he tells everyone *no,* he says *no* to the whole thing. He says *no* several times, enjoying the sound of this word a little more each time he uses it. And then slowly, with more grace than he has ever expected to witness, Claire unwraps her arms from around Ben's waist and backs away from him and Daria is lowered safely back down to the ground.

Cheap Clown

We got the cheap clown. She came without helium, with those sad little balloons you can find in the grocery store. Her shoes fit her feet perfectly, and she didn't even bother to try to pancake over the angry little hickey on her neck. I could go on, but having recently given birth, I lack all but the most base of imaginations.

When the clown finally walked in, fifteen minutes late and without any of the fanfare promised by the more expensive clowns—no musical accompaniment, no unicycle, no rush of confetti—I retreated to my corner of the den and angrily nursed the baby I had spent two and a half hours pushing out just a month before. At first everyone had been excited about all that wet, dark hair. "Push!" they yelled at me. "Just wait until you see all that hair." But toward the end, no one gave a damn. They didn't even count her fingers and toes before laying her panting body on my stomach and moving on. She might have had webbed feet for all they knew. What did they care? They did their job. We were not an easy case. That's the way I thought of us now as I glared at the clown from my corner of the den while my husband ushered her in to meet the birthday boy. We're not easy.

Not like my son, Adam. He had come out faster, even though he was my first baby, all elbows and shoulder blades even then, none of the slow fleshiness of his sister. He loved this clown for coming to his birthday party, believed she was there because he had invited her. Even though I was already soured toward the clown, it still floored me the way he smiled shyly up at her, too awed to even touch her silky, pink pantaloons, which I knew this kid was absolutely dying to do. My son didn't know anything about money yet. He thought grown-ups were motivated strictly by desire because this is what we taught him. *Daddy goes to work because it makes him feel good*, we lied.

This was my husband's, Donny's, clown. On the other hand, this was my house, even the thick varicose vein-shaped crack I suddenly noticed in the corner of the ceiling. We divided things up that way. Next year I got to do the birthday party. The next house was his. The smaller things we weren't so rigid about, not like some of those couples who, even after they are married, still tally their grocery expenses on the refrigerator, tacked there with a magnet for everyone to see. We felt ourselves much superior in this regard. In this regard, we were absolutely together.

*

I wanted to say no to the clown when she came over to my corner to ask if she could lie down for a few minutes in the bedroom. Although we were promised three, she had played only one game with the kids so far and a lame one at that: Pin the Nose on the Clown. She blindfolded the kids with little cardboard masks and spun them around so half-heartedly the larger children didn't even complete full circles and winded up pinning their noses on the wrong wall entirely.

"What about the birthday boy's crown?" I asked.

"Oh, shit," she said. "It's in the car. Do you mind if I get it after I wake up?"

Now the clown didn't just intend to take a break: she planned to take a full-blown nap. She looked stricken, as if she might decide to lie down right there in the den in front of the children any second now, so I led her to our bedroom, absurdly embarrassed that I hadn't bothered to make the bed that morning. The truth was that I hadn't bothered to make the bed any morning since the baby was born.

"Perfect," the clown said, covering herself up with the bedspread.

The baby had fallen asleep in my arms so I put her in the bassinet next to the bed and made the clown promise to listen for her. I left my son's clown in the bedroom and went out to join the birthday party. The doorbell didn't work, so I had purposely propped open the door with one of Donny's shoes so people could let themselves in. But now there was someone yelling "Yoo hoo!" through the crack in the door anyway. I opened the door to the smell of too much vanilla perfume. Rebecca, my son's best friend at preschool, huddled behind her mother, one of the many mothers whose names I could never quite get right.

"Lovely, really lovely," Rebecca's mother said to me. "Just an adorable house."

From what I could tell from her drop-off and pick-up outfits at preschool, this mother had a tendency to overdress for work, but I thought she might have given it a rest on the weekend. Instead she seemed to have made more elaborate choices than ever, wearing pale blue pumps that matched both her earrings and sweater.

Rebecca stuck out a wrapped package from behind her mother's back and I took it and led them both into the den, where several children sat listlessly on the couch. A few limp balloons drifted across the floorboards. My husband, Donny, was kneeling on the ground in front of the children, swinging out his arms in enormous circles in front of him and braying. "Whoever guesses right gets a prize," he said, although I doubted he remembered to buy any prizes. "Come on. Who can guess what kind of animal I am?"

Even though it was his party, it was my idea that the party should remain inside, and now I felt partially responsible for the way inertia had begun to descend upon it. I hated California in July, the rainy season months away and nothing to look forward to each day but more of the sun's unrelenting glare. If it were up to me, we would have held the party closer to sundown when at least the air would have begun to thicken a bit. But this was Donny's party, not mine, and he had chosen its midday time. The only reason he had finally agreed to have it indoors was because I convinced him that the baby had inherited his thin Irish skin and would burn in our shadeless yard.

Now as I watched Donny slowly give up a detailed impersonation of an animal none of the children were correctly guessing, I began to wonder if I should have been so adamant. I considered pulling open the blinds and releasing the stray balloons the clown had left behind into the yard and having the children run out after them. But before I could, Rebecca's mother picked up three thin green balloons and began twisting them furiously.

"Let's see if I remember this right," she said. "The ears are the hardest."

"It's a poodle!" Adam shouted. "You made a poodle."

"I was an elephant," Donny said to Rebecca's mother, "but no one got it. You're obviously far superior in the animal department."

I backed my way out of the den, leaving Donny to charm Rebecca's mother into keeping the rest of the party going. I kept backing down the hallway until I hit my room. I found the clown sitting on my bed, eating earthquake food. Not the family's supply, which my husband had stowed on a shelf in the garage, rotating canned goods every six months the way some book he read told him to, but my private stock that I kept in my end table drawer. Specifically, she had her hand stuck deep into a bag of Crunch and Munch.

"You know you really shouldn't be eating that junk when you're pregnant," I told her.

"Hmm?" she said.

"Or even if you just think you are. Here, I'll take those."

She dropped the bag limply into my hand. "Oh, god," she said. "You probably really want to fire me now." The clown lay back down and swept her hand across her forehead in a dramatic gesture.

My daughter continued to sleep in her bassinet, her lips softly smacking. Air nursing, Donny called it. Her ears were mismatched, not obviously so, one lobe just slightly longer than the other. One day, she'd probably notice this and blame me for my inexact genetics.

"There's a woman in my den making poodles out of your balloons," I said. "She's really very good. You're off the hook for now, I guess." I finished up the Crunch and Munch and lay down next to the clown on my bed, keeping a careful distance.

"I mean I don't even have a real boyfriend anymore," she said. "You're so lucky. All this. What happens if I keep it? What about when I start showing? No one wants to hire a pregnant clown. You have no idea how some of these moms are. Not like you. 'Snow White should be fairer'; 'Jasmine should be darker'; 'Alice should be blonder.' I play them all. Whatever they want. They write letters, for god's sake. They sit down and write goddamn complaint letters. Get a life, is what I say. Get a goddamn life."

"Shh," I told the clown. "You should rest." Mostly, though, I wanted her to be quiet because I was starting to sincerely dislike her. I could hear the party fully underway in the den now. Someone had put on a CD of slightly off-kilter nursery rhymes that my son loves. I could hear him giggling, singing along to a robust and bluesy rendition of "Inky Dinky Spider."

The clown's sleep was not as pretty as my daughter's. Her nose seemed slightly clogged; one of her legs quivered in a heavy spasm under her pantaloons. Still, her arms were long and slim, and her skin looked smooth under all her clown makeup. You could see how a man might have loved her.

I got out of bed and walked over to my window. The street was full of cars I didn't recognize. For a minute, I even forgot which one was mine. Then I spotted the cardboard shade with the huge sunglasses on it that my son, Adam, had picked out. Minutes passed. No one came looking for me.

The clown had left her bag of tricks by the bed. I reached inside and pulled out a long scarf tied to another scarf and another after that. I pulled out four aces of clubs, a thin coloring book with a clown on the cover, a stuffed dime-store bunny, a travel-sized tin of aspirin, a neon pink appointment book. I opened the appointment book and stared at her remaining summer: a Cinderella in July, an Esmeralda in August.

I thought about waking the clown to have a heart-to-heart or at least to fire her, but I didn't do it. The clown and my daughter were both having dreams now. The air was ripe with their private betrayals. In the distance, a freeway I'd never heard before buzzed past.

A Good Bet

Ada feels her heart move. It pushes out like fingers against the inside of her chest. She stops breathing for a moment and lets it pass. There is very little that will not pass. Her granddaughter, she notices, has become an odd attraction. She is six feet tall and wears a vinyl miniskirt that zippers up the back. In the Golden Nugget, their blackjack dealer slows down the turning of his cards to look at Cynthia again. Ada's heart moves back inside where it lives.

"Grandma," Cynthia says, "I'm down to five dollars. Now can we play the slots?"

All evening Cynthia has wanted to play the slots. The slots are the only thing she understands in the casino. Ada worries that her grand-daughter is not that quick. They have spent days preparing, discuss-ing the complexities of blackjack, the possible combinations, when to hit and when to stay. And still, Cynthia doubles-down on a number as uncertain as eight, takes a card on seventeen even though Ada has told her, "Never hit seventeen. Never hit seventeen."

Cynthia has lost Ada's money all night long. The only thing that she hasn't lost is her impatience. The blackjack dealer winks at Cynthia as she turns to walk away and Ada thinks that he has wasted his wink on the wrong person.

"There is no theory at all when it comes to the slot machines," Ada says.

"Good," Cynthia says. She inserts a quarter and pulls at the lever.

*

When they get back to Ada's apartment, Cynthia goes to her bedroom and shuts the door. Ada listens outside. She would be happy to hear anything, but she hears nothing. She knows that Cynthia is standing at the other side of the door, waiting for Ada to leave. Later, if she cannot sleep, Ada will lean out of her bedroom window, as she does most nights, and, unnoticed, will watch Cynthia open her window and practice blowing perfect smoke rings into the sky. "I used to smoke," Ada would like to tell her. Perhaps they could share a cigarette, standing there together in Cynthia's room, by the window.

Ada finally turns away from Cynthia's door, walks down the hallway to her own room, sits on her bed and takes off her blouse. This blouse is one of her favorites. It's made of blue silk. When she lifts it over her head, Ada is left with her old skin. She lies down on the bed and touches herself between her breasts, where her heart is. Although she knows better, she imagines her heart to be heart-shaped, like a valentine.

Ada lines up her bottles of pills across the top of her night table. She studies the labels' complicated instructions: Take one three times a day before meals, take two twice a day after eating, take one every night before bed, take half a tablet twice a day with water. Then she frowns, closes her eyes, and reaches for one bottle, then another. She takes two pills from each of the two bottles that she has chosen, then puts the pill bottles away.

Ada picks up the phone when Phil calls to check in. She would like to tell him the truth, that his daughter is sullen and lacks the ability to concentrate. But Phil already has enough problems. "We went to the movies tonight," Ada lies. "Something with John Wayne in it. Something about the west."

This seems to satisfy Phil. Ada can tell because he is quiet after she says it.

"She's a good girl," Ada says.

"That's good," Phil says. "John Wayne is good."

When Phil hangs up, Ada is alone with her heart again. But her heart is quiet. She takes the stethoscope that she stole from her last doctor out of her night table drawer and listens to the pounding, the everydayness of it, until she falls asleep.

*

The next day while Ada is eating lunch, Cynthia brings home a boy from the beach. The boy is wearing long, floral swim trunks and no T-shirt. He is very polite, however. He tells Ada that he likes old people. "I bet you're full of stories," he says. "I love old people like you."

Studying her reflection in the silver serving platter on top of Ada's breakfront, Cynthia practices her closed-mouth disagreeableness.

Ada would like to please this boy, but when she tries to think of a story to tell him, she is blank. From a talk show that morning she'd discovered how children with homosexual parents learn to adapt, but she thinks that this is not the kind of story the boy wants to hear. "Did you wash off your feet? I don't want sand in this apartment," she says instead.

Cynthia sighs and turns reluctantly away from her reflection to look at her grandmother. "You're hopeless," she says. "Come on, Billy. Forget lunch. Let's get out of here."

When Ada is alone again, she clears her dishes and washes them off in the kitchen sink. "You kids have fun," she says now that it's too late. Then she goes to her bedroom to think. That night when Phil calls, she will tell him that Cynthia finally made a friend, a girl with nice manners, a girl with no sand on her feet.

But when Phil calls, she doesn't say this. He calls at a bad moment. Ada is washing her underwear in the bathtub, a slow and soothing and rhythmic act, and one from which she does not appreciate being interrupted. "You've raised a slut," she says.

"Shit," Phil says. "Tell me what medication you're on. Did you miss any of your pills again?"

"No," Ada lies. She reads the labels on her pill bottles to Phil. She recites the foreign-sounding words.

"Check," Phil says, after she reads each label. "Check, check, check."

"She's a ditz like miss-you-know-who."

"Mother," Phil says, "do you know what I'm doing right now? I'm sitting here at the kitchen table, and I'm eating bologna. There are brown spots on the bologna. I don't need this."

"You had a mother. Didn't I teach you anything? Eat something else for God's sake."

"There's nothing else to eat," Phil says. "She took the goddamn car. There's no car pool to the supermarket. You want me to take the bus, a bus full of Hispanics? I'd rather eat the bologna. I'd rather not give her the satisfaction."

"Get with the program, Phil. Adapt. Even children with homosexual parents learn to adapt," Ada says. Secretly, Ada sides with Phil's wife, Beth. Even if she does have her head up in the clouds, at least Beth had enough spunk to take the car.

Ada opens her night table drawer and takes out the stethoscope. When she puts the soft rubber ends of it in her ears, she cannot hear her son. When she holds the round metal end of it to the phone, she hears the buzzing aftermath of someone else's conversation coming at her from far away.

*

When Cynthia gets home at three A.M., Ada is waiting for her in Cynthia's room, the room where Ada's husband hid when he wanted to escape her. Her husband called the room his study, but he kept a bed in it, too. After he died Ada went through his desk drawers hoping to find a secret bank account, a record of his bets at the races, even love letters to another woman. Anything. But the drawers were those found in a hotel room desk. Stationary, a Bible, three pens, an unopened package of envelopes. A clean exit. Nothing. When Cynthia comes home, Ada is sitting on his bed.

"I guess I should have called, right?" Cynthia says.

"You're such a tall girl," Ada says. "They didn't used to make girls so tall when I was a girl."

Cynthia laughs, and this is one of the few times all month that Ada has clearly seen the braces across her granddaughter's teeth. The braces are shiny and delicate-looking, and Ada can't imagine why Cynthia has tried to keep them hidden from her for so long.

When Ada doesn't move, Cynthia fakes a yawn and begins undressing in front of her. She sits down on the floor and unlaces her sneakers. She turns her jeans inside out and pulls them off her feet, lifts her T-shirt over her head. She steps out of her bathing suit, and specks of sand fly through the air. Then she says, "excuse me," and walks naked by her grandmother. She opens a dresser drawer and slips another, larger T-shirt over her head.

Ada is very patient. She could sit here all night. "I could sit here all night," she says.

"Grandma," Cynthia says, "don't you think it's time for both of us to go to bed now?"

"You should put yourself on a pedestal with that boy," Ada says.

"Jesus, Grandma. What are you talking about?"

Ada isn't really sure, but it seemed like grandmotherly advice when she said it. It's something that her grandmother or someone like her grandmother told her.

Ada sits, trying to figure out what she was talking about, and Cynthia paces the room, picking up the clothes she has dropped on the floor.

"Your mother," Ada says, "she used to be a very nice girl before you knew her. She made a coffee cake for me once. It was a funny cake, but she tried. There was soft dough in the middle of it. I don't think your father had any. He was never much for sweets."

"I don't want to talk about her," Cynthia says.

"Of course not. Let me show you something," Ada says. "You wait here. I'll be right back." Ada hurries to her bedroom and brings back the pearls and the stethoscope. "These," she says, holding out the pearls, "will be yours when I'm dead."

Cynthia loops the pearls three times around her bony wrist, like a bracelet. "Are they real?" she says.

"Yes," Ada says. "Certainly."

"Wow," Cynthia says.

"Now I want to listen," Ada says. She pats the space next to her on the bed. Cynthia looks quickly around the room. She finds the open door, touches the pearls wrapped around her wrist and finally sits down on the bedspread beside her grandmother.

Ada smiles, places the soft rubber plugs in her ears and holds the round metal end of the stethoscope against her granddaughter's chest. She listens. She waits. Her granddaughter's heart is strong and steady. If Cynthia allowed her to, Ada could sit here all night.

You Can't Dance

All night long Jenny has been trying to get me to dance with her. She gives me the choice of either dancing or agreeing to do one other thing for her without objection. At first we are inside, in her living room, surrounded by all of the things I hope one day to forget: the frail-looking porcelain doll carrying the basket of gold and blue silk flowers, the arched arms of the wicker couch, the Mexican vase that I gave her for her birthday.

When I go out to the patio to smoke, she follows me with her tape player, sets it down and turns up the volume. We have already been through the fifties and sixties and now we are on the seventies, "Stayin' Alive," and Jenny's hips moving from side to side in front of me.

"I think you've had enough to drink," I say.

"Now you think so," she says. "You couldn't wait for me to get drunk."

"I thought you could use one drink," I say. "I didn't mean for you to get drunk."

"I'm not drunk anyway," she says, grabbing my hands and trying to pull me up off of the stoop. "Come on, do the one thing for me or just dance."

This is tough, but I know it could be worse, so finally I stand up and move around a little, swing my arms back and forth as if I were walking without legs.

*

Before Jenny's mother died, Jenny and I met at a motel called the Lucky Seven. The motel was shaped like a horseshoe, and in our room the bathroom was separated by a partition instead of a wall. I would lie in bed and listen to Jenny pee before she came in to me. Sometimes she would go into the bathroom and I would hear nothing at all. "Please, Jenny," I'd say, standing by the bathroom door. "Come on out now." And she would. There was a question, but there was never a scene.

This is the first scene. Tonight. At her house. Dancing with Jenny on the patio. Sometimes the bug light zaps something. The zap sounds like a forgotten note, something on the keyboard maybe, a tiny cymbal on the drum.

At first I refused to come to her house. At first she didn't ask. And then when her mother got worse and Jenny did ask, I refused. I'd want to meet her farther and farther away. Over the phone I would give her subway and bus directions, and on the outskirts of the city we would meet at a restaurant. Because she wouldn't order, I would order for her. I wanted her to eat. She seemed undernourished. I would order crabmeat crepes for her and make her finish them, even the sprig of parsley because parsley is a vegetable, and parsley has vitamins. "Eat the parsley, Jenny," I would say.

*

At home my wife Lillian is painting a picture because this is what she does, paints. She finds pictures of exotic-looking places in Africa in the encyclopedia, and in high-school history textbooks left over from when she taught high school, and in the history textbooks that I still use to teach, and she paints them. Sometimes she adds people for variety—women with long, mutilated earlobes, thick hoops of silver around their necks. Once she even had a show. It was on the second level of a gallery. I sipped wine and pretended to be very proud of her. Lillian wore a dashiki. Once, before I knew her, she went to Africa on a safari with a group of schoolteachers from around the country who were chosen because of their teaching skills.

It was at Lillian's show that I met Jenny. She was there for another exhibit, a photography show that was opening simultaneously. The photography show was downstairs, and when I passed through it to step outside and smoke, I saw Jenny holding up a small magnifying glass to a photograph of a dog, lying on its back, hidden in high grass. Later she told me that she was studying the grain.

*

When the tape ends, Jenny does not flip it over. She sits on the stoop next to me, and this is when, I hope, it will finally begin to be over.

"What I don't understand," she says, "is why you want to leave me now. Now is when I need you."

"I know," I say. "I'm a bastard. Let it alone at that. Okay?"

"No, not okay," she says. "Absolutely not okay."

"I'm not who you need right now," I say. "How about your sister? You told me that you've always been close to your sister."

"Got along with," she says. "Not close. It's not the same thing."

"In any case, I think it would be a good idea if you went to stay with her for a while. She invited you, right? She's married, and she even has a guest room, right?"

"Jesus, William," she says, "I can't accept this. I really can't. I don't know how you expect me to accept this."

"I want you to hate me," I say. "That's what I deserve. I want you to hate me."

Jenny gets up and goes inside the house. She comes out with another tape and slips it on. Elvis Presley. This is very bad. It really is. We're back to the fifties again, and Elvis Presley seems like a very bad sign.

When Jenny dances this time, there is nothing pretty about it. She kicks her feet out in front of her. She grabs a handful of air, pretends it's a microphone and sings right along.

It wasn't always this way with us. In the beginning she never asked me to come to her house. We met at the Lucky Seven. It was shaped like a horseshoe. Sometimes I would listen to Jenny pee, and I thought that was what love was like, lying there, waiting.

At home my wife Lillian would be painting. Sometimes she would call our son Edward at school, and when I got home from the Lucky Seven she would tell me all about his faraway life, a life that made no sense to me. He lived off-campus and had a girlfriend. His girlfriend was an art major. Didn't I think that was something, Lillian would ask me, the way kids mimic their parents' lives without even realizing it?

Last weekend when we went up to visit Edward, and Jenny went to her mother's funeral, I decided then what I knew all along, that I would have to tell Jenny that there would be an ending, that the ending would not be some faraway thing that was impossible to understand, that I would become the enemy, the one who pressed for closure.

*

When Jenny goes into the house again, I take the batteries out of the tape player and put them in my shirt pocket. All night long there has been music and Jenny dancing and me sitting and getting up and trying to explain about how real life is such a sudden and horrible thing. I have been sounding like a married man, an older man, something I am, somebody who could not stand by Jenny's mother's grave and hold Jenny's hand while she cried because her mother had died of a cancer that came out of nowhere and ate its way through her pancreas.

At the photography show when Jenny was studying the grain, I saw her back and the way her hair curled away from it as if it didn't really end, but grew back into itself. "Are you the photographer?" I said.

"No, I live near here. I was just passing by. I'm only studying the grain," she said. "Would you like to have a look?"

When we got home Lillian was very excited. This was before the reviewer wrote the small blurb saying that her art was racist. She wanted to talk about all the people who had come to her show, how many of them we didn't even know, that were interested purely in her work. I opened a bottle of champagne, and at the kitchen table she toasted, one at time, each stranger that showed up for her opening whose face she could remember.

*

"Why won't you do one last thing for me?" Jenny says.

"Okay, I'll do it," I say. She is standing in the doorway to the patio, and when I look up at her, I see the tiny blond hairs on her legs, illuminated by the incandescent kitchen light. It is all I can do to remember that I am the enemy and not pull her down next to me, grab her around the knees so she folds inward toward me, so that the length of her collapses.

At the restaurants we would go to, I always wanted her to eat everything on her plate. Her mother's pancreas was eaten away by a cancer that came out of nowhere. I would even make her eat the small orange slice next to the parsley, because orange is a fruit and orange has vitamins. "Eat your orange, Jenny," I would say. "Oranges are good for you."

"What do you want me to do?" I say.

"Come inside," she says. "I'll show you."

I follow Jenny inside through her kitchen, upstairs into her bathroom that is small and papered with tiny purple flowers on a white background.

"Stand in the shower," she says. "It's all right. You can keep your clothes on."

I slide open the shower door and stand inside, being careful not to knock over the row of bottles of shampoo and conditioner on the window ledge, feeling as if it is important not to leave fingerprints. "Have you even had dinner?" I say. "Maybe we should get something to eat."

"Shh," Jenny says. "Can't you see I'm doing something?"

Jenny is sitting on the floor going through the cabinet under the sink. Ridiculously, with all my clothes on, with my shoes on, I am standing in her shower.

*

It wasn't always this way. I never expected it to get this way. We used to meet at the Lucky Seven Motel. The bathroom there was separated only by a partition. We were never in it together. I would lie in bed waiting, thinking that she would never come out, that I would never know what love is.

At home my wife Lillian would be painting. Once she went through my journal, and when I got home she told me that I could never be a painter, that it was impossible to even imagine hair that grew back into itself that way. I told Lillian that there would be a closure, and she said that she would wait for it. For years we had each waited out many things that ended. Our son was off at college, off-campus. Lillian rubbed lotion on my shoulders while I lay on my stomach in bed and cried. Jenny's mother's pancreas was eaten away by a cancer. Once she showed me a picture of her mother, and she didn't look at all like Jenny, but I said yes, that she did. Lillian leaned over me in a nightgown that was familiar, a nightgown that smelled like sheets, and I pulled her down to me.

"I found it," Jenny says, standing up.

"This isn't right," I say. "I'm getting out of the shower now."

"You promised one last thing," Jenny says. "You said okay." Jenny unscrews the top to a jar of black shoe polish and dips a finger in it. "I just want to see what you used to look like when you were younger," she says, smoothing the polish back into my hair.

My hair feels heavy, like molasses, when she pulls the comb through it. "Will this come out?" I say.

"It'll come out. Just shampoo it. Really."

I step out of the shower and stand where Jenny positions me in front of the bathroom mirror. "My hair was never this black," I say.

"You told me it was black," she says.

"Well, it wasn't like this. It must have been dark brown. You're drunk. I think you should eat. Are you sure you don't want to get something to eat?"

"You look handsome, I think," Jenny says.

"Thank you," I say.

"It's okay. That's all. I just wanted to see."

I walk downstairs and wash my hair out with dish soap in the kitchen sink. The batteries from my pocket fall out onto the floor. I walk outside to Jenny's patio and put them back in her tape recorder.

"I've got to leave now," I shout up the stairs.

Jenny comes down the stairs and looks at me standing by her front door.

"I'm sorry," I say. "I'm sorry about your mother and about this. I want you to find someone else. You're very young. You'll see."

"I just wanted to see what you used to look like. It's okay. That's all I wanted. I didn't even want you to dance. You're a very bad dancer. I'm surprised how bad you are. You can go now."

It wasn't always this way. When I saw her studying the grain, I thought that her hair curled back into itself. Outside she smoked my cigarette, and neither one of us talked about our lives.

My Treat, Geronimo

When I see a child like this, there is only one thing I can think: What are his parents like? Since my husband, Louis, died, I've seen plenty. For the past two years, I've ridden the train from Baltimore to D.C. because I never did learn how to drive, and I don't care what my daughter says, sixty-five is too old to start learning something mechanical, especially when your health is privately failing. Not that an older person can't learn other things. They make black baby dolls for children now. Asian ones, too. This, for example, is something I didn't previously know. I saw a little black one just today in the lobby of the train station, its arms open to the sides, lying flat out on a seat.

And I've learned a few things about traveling. Like if you have to wait too long for someone to get out of the ladies' room on a train, you don't want to go in it. What you want to do instead is move right along to the next car and use that ladies' room instead. And if the train looks like it's going to fill up at the next stop, you're better off going ahead and choosing the person you're going to sit next to instead of waiting like a victim for someone to choose you.

The sleeping child in the aisle seat I scooted by is wearing a vinyl jacket that's too small for him and ripped open at the elbow to boot, a patch of bright blue shirt showing through. His mouth is open in sleep, his nose running. I reach in my purse for a tissue and then stop. If you've ever been a mother, there are some gestures you can never quite stop yourself from making. But I have been accused of being too familiar with strangers, so I stop myself. By the time you are my age, believe me, you have been accused of plenty of things especially if you have children, so I've had to pick and choose what to take to heart.

My daughter, Jessica, who I'm on my way to visit, lives in a townhouse she rents for half the going rate because the owners are renovating it while she's living there, getting ready to sell it out from under her. Because of this fact, when she says to me that they've just installed a skylight, I do not allow myself to have visions of pale light pouring down through the roof onto the staircase. What I see instead are my daughter's suitcases on the street.

Since she moved to Washington fourteen years ago, my daughter has lived in twelve different buildings, house-sitting while professors spent semesters abroad and paying next to nothing to keep up appearances for prospective buyers of buildings about to be foreclosed upon. At least she's kept the same job at the American Automotive Leasing Association, where, instead of a cubicle in the main room, she now has her own office with a door she can shut anytime she feels like it. Not to mention the kind of medical benefits that can set a mother's mind at ease.

I touch my foot under the seat in front of me where I have hidden a bag of jelly donuts. According to Jessica, there is not one decent bakery in the entire city of Washington. Like an old lady, she now loves places that she hated when she was growing up. A dusty shoe store she would never sit still in, the soda fountain at Woolco where I always made her order milk instead of floats, and the donut shop we went to maybe a grand total of five times are now all mythic for my daughter. And then there are the places she claims to miss that don't even exist, that never existed in Baltimore, a tropical fish store managed by a Mr. Murphy, an old lot behind our first house, filled with abandoned children's bicycles.

But Jessica always has had trouble with what you and I might call normal reality. When she was a baby we thought she might turn out to be a genius, that's how quickly she learned to talk and make up stories. The summer she was two and a half, she impressed Louis's entire office at a company picnic by acting out all the major roles in *West Side Story*. But she was slower in other ways, not learning to tie her own shoes until she was nearly seven and never figuring out the right way to play with the developmental toys I ordered for her from a special gifted children's catalog, filling empty pretzel tins with the pegs she was supposed to line up by color and height.

So we gave up on the genius idea and tried to give her a normal childhood. People say you always make the most mistakes with your first, but what about your only? Still, maybe it was heredity as much as anything we did. Even though I wouldn't let that woman stay in my house for more than two nights in a row, Jessica went and took after Louis's sister Peggy—Peggy who never got married, whose idea of normal conversation was quizzing someone on presidential running mates from two decades ago, who stared so hard at things sometimes they had to move just to get out of her sight.

*

The little boy sleeping next to me is starting to wake up now, his lips touching together and opening in that fish-like way young children have. I decide he's eight, maybe nine. He wipes his nose with the sleeve of his jacket and blinks at me.

"We're almost there," I say to him.

He looks at me, confused.

"The window seat was empty so I just squished right by while you were sleeping," I tell him. "Crowded today."

He looks around at all the other people reading or sleeping or just staring off like zombies the way so many people do when they have any extra time on their hands like it never crossed their minds they might try doing something useful like knitting or even working through a crossword puzzle, which I certainly did before the headaches began coming on. His straight black bangs, which need, in my opinion, to be trimmed, cover his eyebrows. I resist the temptation to brush them out of his face and instead look at him and try to figure out this thing I was wondering about. About his color, that is. He's not black but he's foreign looking, some kind of Spanish is my guess. Medium brown with a small runny nose and wide eyes, like the kid I sat next to in the waiting room at the oncology department of the hospital just ten days ago, like a child in a magazine you could feed for just ten dollars a month.

"Would you like a jelly donut?" I ask. I reach under the seat in front of me for the bag. They gave me thirteen, a baker's dozen, so I decide it's okay to give him one, that Jessica won't notice the difference.

He thanks me and eats carefully, biting a piece off and sucking the jelly quietly out of the center.

I ask him if he's traveling alone, and he nods.

"What's your name?" I ask.

"Geronimo," he says.

I laugh and he looks at me squarely.

"I'm sorry," I say. "I had no business laughing. That's a fine name. Still, your mother really shouldn't let you travel all this way alone," I say, putting the bag of jelly donuts back under the seat in front of me and almost adding that she should have taught him not to take food from strangers while she was at it. "Where did you get on?"

"Springfield, in Massachusetts. That's nearby where I live at. I'm going to visit my uncle. For a whole month."

We pull into Union Station before I can ask him how he feels about being away from home for so long, and the conductor's voice is garbled in an old P.A. system, so I tell Geronimo that this is our stop and help him get his suitcase down off the rack. It's an old-fashioned hard case, the kind that looks like it might carry a typewriter instead of clothes. As I follow him down the aisle, I decide he looks like one of the little, hunched-over old people who shuffled down the hallway at the nursing home where Louis went after his stroke.

Outside Union Station, we wait and wait for his ride. I do not plan to leave him alone, so I pretend I'm waiting for someone, too, in the noonday sun, even though I always take a taxi to Jessica's house since, although she can drive, she's never had a car.

"I think there's been a mistake," Geronimo finally says.

"Do you think your uncle has the wrong time?" I ask.

"Where are all the palm trees at?" Geronimo asks.

"There aren't any palm trees in Washington," I tell him.

"See what I mean about there being a mistake. I didn't think this was Miami," he says.

"Of course this isn't Miami," I say, shooing a fly away from my jelly donut bag. "Oh my God," I say as it hits me that I've led him off the train at the wrong stop. I rush with him back inside, but we're too late. Our train has already pulled out, and we have four hours until the next one leaves for Miami. "Let's have a nice lunch," I tell him as we sit on a bench outside and go over the schedule. "You can call your uncle and tell him you stopped to visit a friend of your mother's in Washington and you'll be right along."

"But my mom doesn't know no one in Washington," he says.

And then I see it coming, his eyes filling up with tears, his nose starting to run again. "Oh, Geronimo, honey, it's okay," I say. "Please, have another jelly-filled to tide you over." The first one I grab for squirts open in my fingers. I hold open the bag for him, and he peers inside and delicately picks one out.

In the cab, I give him a tissue and tell him that as soon as we get to Jessica's we'll call his uncle and tell him what happened. I talk non-stop, the way Jessica tells me I always do when I'm nervous. I tell him about how pretty my daughter's house is even though I can barely remember this one, how the sun streams right in through the skylight onto the wood stairs.

When Jessica answers the door wearing the red kimono she has an unfortunate tendency to live in on the weekends, I put my finger to my lips so she won't ask a lot of questions. I don't want to scare Geronimo anymore than he already is.

Geronimo speaks in Spanish on the phone to his uncle. I can hear the uncle's voice louder than I can hear Geronimo's even though I am standing right next to him. Geronimo hands the phone to me and says, "Explain to him," and in careful, slow sentences I do my best.

"We don't have any money to pay for a kidnapping," his uncle tells me in surprisingly good English when I finish talking.

"Of course not," I say. "Geronimo will be there on the eleven-forty five."

Jessica says, "Well, well, well," when I hang up the phone. "Nice going, Mother." Then she moves right along. "Did you bring me those donuts? I've been thinking about them all morning long."

"I promised Geronimo a nice lunch to make up for my little mistake, so don't eat them all right now," I say, handing her the bag.

"Yuck, I wanted Bavarian creme. There's jelly squirted everywhere. How could you forget? We always got the Bavarian."

I don't know what to say, whether to pretend that I'm wrong when I know I specifically heard her say *jelly*, or to confront her with the truth. Probably she's construed a whole series of memories around the Bavarian creme. God only knows.

"You take them, then, Geronimo," I say, taking the bag from my daughter and handing it to him. "Eat them if you get hungry later on the way to Florida. Jessica, now show us what they've done around here."

My daughter moves slowly, pointing out the small detail work, the beaded wood by the staircase where the paint has been peeled away. She bends over and I look at the split ends of her brown hair, resist touching her slim shoulder blades that poke out against her kimono, even though we both know I created those blades with my own body. She could be so pretty is what I think, if only she could pull herself together a little but already thirty-four now, I don't see this happening. The thing about having a daughter like Jessica is it's not so hard to imagine her growing old alone the way it might be with some other kind of child. A long time ago, I decided to pretend that my daughter was like some traveling salesman who lived her life out of hotel rooms. Except in her case she never actually travels anywhere. I don't even bother looking around the townhouse for clues about her life. I know without looking that the black-and-white prints on the wall won't have any people in them that have any real relationship to my daughter.

Halfway up the stairs my head begins to ache, and I think about the prescription in my pocketbook but keep walking. Geronimo taps me on the back and points up to the skylight. The glass is striped yellow, blue, and pink, and the afternoon sun shining through has left a rainbow on the stairway wall. "Oh, that's pretty," I say.

"One month," Jessica says, "and then I'm out of here."

Jessica goes to her room and changes into a long, black, robe-like dress and ropy sandals, an outfit that doesn't look to me much more suited for leaving the house in than her kimono, but I don't say a word. Like I said, a mother learns when to keep her mouth shut. Besides, what do I know about fashion? It's summer so I'm wearing one of the sleeveless dresses a person accumulates over the years, despite the fact that my arms are meatier than they used to be. We walk over to a restaurant with a neon sign that reads *Flamingos*, Geronimo trudging behind us with his little suitcase. We sit out front on the patio. The waiters are talking in what sounds like Spanish to each other, and I ask Geronimo if he can understand them.

"Mother, that's Portuguese. How could he understand?" Jessica says, smoothing down an invisible wrinkle in her sleeve. "Honestly. Someone needs a serious geography lesson."

Although this isn't a pretty thing to admit, the truth is, although I try my best, I don't always like my daughter. This is not to say she isn't capable of impressing me. After years of living on her own in the city, Jessica knows much more about foreign cuisine than I've ever hoped to learn. I tell her to order for us, and the three of us eat quietly, watching people walk by in pairs and small groups. Several times I try to start conversations but have trouble locating a topic the three of us can sustain for more than two sentences. Finally, I give up and let this still-new dizziness set in. It isn't unpleasant, really, feeling so off-balance. It reminds me of being pregnant with Jessica, of standing up too quickly after a bath and having to lie down wet on top of the bed afterward, not even worrying for once in my life about the bedspread.

After lunch, we walk around Dupont Circle looking in store windows because we still have nearly two hours until Geronimo's train leaves. That's when I get my idea. "Geronimo, how about we surprise your uncle by getting you a nice haircut?" I say.

With his free hand, Geronimo touches the back of his head. "But my mother always does it," he tells me.

"Even so, it looks like it's been a while," I say. "Come on. My treat. Let me pay for it to make up for the inconvenience I've caused."

He shrugs and I take this for a yes. I ignore Jessica's audible sighs and lead them both into the beauty parlor that had caught my eye. Inside, it doesn't disappoint. Unlike most of the places Jessica takes me on my visits, there is nothing at all modern or sophisticated about House of Style. The comforting smell of aerosol hairspray fills the air. The stylists wear white smocks and flat shoes with spongy soles. I take a chance. "This reminds me of Dee Dees. Remember, honey? You used to beg to go with me to have my hair set and styled before one of Daddy's big company dinners."

"Hmm," Jessica says, apparently considering the idea. "I guess it does have that kind of feel to it."

I give the receptionist Geronimo's name and flip through hairstyling magazines while we wait. Furtively, I glance at my daughter, several chairs away reading *Newsweek* as if by herself, and in my mind's eye try several fluffy, highlighted styles on her conservatively bobbed head. I barely notice how quiet Geronimo is in the chair next to me until his name is called and he still doesn't move. "That's you, honey," I say.

"Just my mom's done it forever," he says.

"Oh, that's fine," I say. "They're very nice here, really. Just like your mom but with professional scissors. Maybe they'll even give you a treat afterward."

Stoically, Geronimo follows the stout young woman who's called his name. I watch him shiver as she hooks a bib around his neck. "What'll be, Grandma?" she calls to me.

I consider correcting her but think better of it. I walk over to the chair and allow myself the gesture I resisted earlier that day. Gently, I push Geronimo's bangs to the side, out of his eyes. "He has such beautiful eyes. Let's have a look at them," I tell her. I stand close by and watch her cut the hair of this boy whose last name I don't even know. I rub his shoulder for reassurance, hold up the hand mirror so he can see the back when she finally turns him around to inspect.

After Geronimo's haircut, Jessica comes with us to Union Station to wait for the train. All three of us wind up in the back seat of the cab, Geronimo in the middle, like he might really be Jessica's son, my grandson. His small suitcase and the bag of donuts are set carefully on his lap. I silently practice the sentence I am slowly realizing I will never say aloud to my daughter. *A tumor the size of a small lime has settled next to my brain.* Although I had planned on living at least ten years longer, I have decided that sixty-five will have to do.

According to the electronic display I have become adept at scanning, the train Geronimo needs to be on is running half an hour late. I give him a handful of quarters, and he calls his uncle from a phone booth. When he puts me on the line this time, his uncle says, "I hope you're a decent lady, a woman of your word. We can get some money if that's what it takes. So far, I've spared his mother."

"Of course," I say. "No, I mean. No money, really. It was just an honest mistake." I give the uncle the new arrival time and return to the bench where Jessica and Geronimo are waiting.

"It's fine," I tell them. "Everything's been ironed out."

"Okay," Geronimo says. He yawns and then snaps open his suitcase, reaches his hand under neatly folded T-shirts, and pulls out two small, plastic dolls wearing capes and smashes them together several times. His new haircut gives him a raw, startled look. A light red rash has broken out at the back of his neck where they shaved the hair away from his collar. "Bam, whack him, boom," Geronimo says.

Jessica and I stand together watching long after Geronimo has walked down the ramp that takes him to his train. My daughter is standing so close to me that I can feel her sleeve touch my bare arm. In Geronimo's pocket is my phone number, although I don't expect he will really call me when he gets to Florida. Why should he? All around us, people hurry by. If you've ever been a mother, you know how hard this kind of moment can be, even when it's not your goodbye to say.

 Aghast

I see the fat lady smoking and I think this: she doesn't have too long for this world. She smokes so comfortably it's like we're in a neighborhood bar, but we're outside, all gathered together around the police barricade, watching. I'm right up front and the fat lady is next to me. When she drops her cigarette and looks down to step on it, that's when she notices me. I stare up at her, daring her to have a reaction to my size, and she shakes her head a little as if she's saying *no* and then looks back out at the action again.

A pretty girl with dark brown hair curled around her shoulders is running down Royal Street, chasing after a man who has stolen her purse. The street is closed off for five blocks. I feel like shouting, "shoot the bastard!"—this to the guy chasing after the girl who is chasing the guy who stole her purse. But if I do, one of the police standing inside the barricade will step over the red ribbon I'm looking under and will ask me to leave. Only the extras are allowed to shout and only some of them.

Marla is supposed to look aghast. "Aghast," she told me, as if the word itself conjured up every possible image of Hollywood, as if Marla had been blessed by an assistant director with this one word. Marla is inside the barricade, across the street, gazing in an antique store window, trying to catch the angle of her face reflected in it in such a way that the reflection will show up on TV, in case when the girl runs past her and Marla finally turns around to notice, they edit Marla out or her face gets lost in the myriad extra faces.

And now it's Marla's turn to notice, and I watch as she turns slowly from the store window for the third time this afternoon, as her jaw slackens and her face gets longer and her eyeballs roll up toward her forehead, aghast. And I'm not even sure where the camera is when Marla is aghast, where it is pointed. It's on a little platform with a motor and while the driver's moving the platform, the cameraman is focusing. I hope that he catches Marla this way, with her face long and a little crazy. I hope that in a month we can turn on the TV at two and Marla will see herself there, and then we can replay this whole afternoon together, everything that is happening at this moment.

The fat lady next to me lights another cigarette and looks at me like she wants to sit down. She looks at me as if maybe I could excuse my little self and give her room to sit or maybe squat some and offer myself up as a chair to her. This time I shake my head at her, and she blows her cigarette smoke up in the air and sighs as if life were too exhausting to do more than this.

*

When they chose Marla for an extra, we celebrated, Marla and I, with champagne I got from the restaurant where I work four nights a week. I wear a tuxedo and ride a unicycle between the tables, carrying roses in my teeth, offering them to the ladies. Although it would be easy to find this job humiliating, I see it, with the tips, as a way to make decent money. The restaurant I work at is one of those theme restaurants for tourists. The food is named after Mardi Gras krewes— Chicken Zulu, Bacchus Burgers, Proteus Pie. The waitresses wear fishnet stockings and spray-painted gold feathers in their hair. Marla works there too, as a waitress, but she has other ambitions. Mostly she just wants to be famous in some way so she can impress her parents in Ohio who think she's screwed up everything since the day she left home.

When she got the role, Marla wanted to call someone, but when she opened her address book and looked through it, she said there was no one to call.

"Tell me again," I said. "You can tell me again, just as if you were telling me for the first time."

"It's not the same. We both know that you already know."

So we drank our champagne and watched television in bed, and Marla compared her face to the face of every actress on television, touching her jaw and eyelashes as if she were trying to make sense out of something. "I think it's better this way," she said, "not telling any-one, just letting them see me on TV and thinking 'I know that girl from someplace.'"

I touched Marla's arm, feeling her cool, freckled skin through her gauze shirt, and she pulled away from me. This was the way it went sometimes. We'd wait until the lights were out. Face it, I'm not her dream man, but we're happy enough in the dark together. I lit a ciga-rette, and Marla said, "Watch it. You'll stunt your growth that way," the old joke between us.

The reception on the TV went bad, and Marla knocked hard on the wall behind our bed at the twins in the apartment next to ours. "You old farts," she said. "Stop playing with the antenna." She blamed the twins for our bad reception, although our building didn't even have an antenna on the roof. It was just one of the things that Marla got in her head and refused to be talked out of.

"Freaks," the twins shouted together. The twins weren't really twins, we just called them that because they did nearly everything in unison, walking to work together with identical home-perms, even bringing men home to their queen-sized bed. When they got men in there, which wasn't often since the twins were somewhat man-like in stature, our whole apartment seemed to shake from it. Marla would be quiet then, turning down the volume on the TV and lying in bed with her head propped up on three pillows, listening.

"This is a bad sign," Marla said, "the reception going fuzzy this way, those damn twins interfering in our lives all the time. Just turn off the TV, Stu. I want to go to sleep."

*

Now all the actors and extras are taking their places again. Although the previous takes seemed smooth enough to me, the director shook his head after each and whispered to the pretty girl, kneading his fingers into her shoulder while he talked to her. Marla is patting her hair down in her reflection in the shop window. Her hair is frizzed from the humidity, and the hairspray we misted it with this morning has made the frizz stiffen around her head in little auburn spikes. A lot of the extras look angry, but not Marla. She pats her hair down and thinks she's going to do aghast the way it's supposed to be done this time. At least that's what she looks like she's thinking.

This time the girl seems to be running faster, too fast, as if she's running away from the man who's behind her, the good guy, the guy who's supposed to be helping her get back her purse from the man who stole it. Marla says the plotline is much more complicated than what I'm watching, that it has to do with drug smuggling, drugs hidden in the bases of stolen heirloom lamps. She knows this not because they've filled in the extras, but because she actually watches this show and has seen the plotlines gathering, leading up to this chase. She's told me the story of the whole missing month, the month that will be shown before they get to this scene, all of her predictions about what will have happened first.

"Stop, thief!" someone shouts, and because I have been busy watching the pretty girl running down Royal Street faster than she was before and wondering if this is what the director wanted or if she is only trying to finally get this scene done with, I realize that I have not been watching Marla, and I look at her. "Stop, thief!" Marla shouts again, getting angry this time, jumping up and down in place, looking like she really means it.

"I don't remember that from before," the fat woman says, looking down at me this time as if I were a friend. "Do you?"

"Shit," I say. "That does it."

— 120

"You don't have to be nasty. We've all been suffering in this heat for the same amount of time."

I'm grateful that it's an assistant director and not a cop who escorts Marla out of the street. She's talking to him while he's leading her away, talking in a quiet, confidential tone, I can tell. I can't hear what Marla's saying, not with the pretty girl screaming at the director about goddamn on-location shooting, but I've seen Marla get this way before, insistent and patient like when she's on the phone with her mother explaining to her why she can't make it home for Christmas.

I push my way back through the crowd and find Marla sitting by herself on the curb, holding her face in her hands, her thumbs up next to her ears like sideburns. "Hey," I say. "It's okay."

"I went with my instincts. I did. That's what I was telling the man. I felt a need for someone to shout that. Don't you think someone should have shouted that? 'Stop, thief.' Someone should always shout 'stop, thief' when there's a mugging."

I sit down next to her and think about that. "You were supposed to look aghast. Remember? You did aghast very well, I thought. You should have stayed with it."

"Let's go home," Marla says. "I'm tired."

Marla and I walk home through the streets that seem deserted to me compared to the crowds around Royal Street. I don't want to get there too fast. I don't want to get in bed with Marla while it's still daylight and lie there and listen to her explain why she did what she did while we watch television and wait for the twins to come home so Marla can bang on the wall at them. So when she makes me stop with her to look in a store window, I feel thankful for the diversion. There's my reflection a foot and a half shorter than Marla's. I turn away from it quickly and look up at Marla's reflection. Her mouth is open and her eyeballs are rolling up, way up past her forehead now, back up inside.

Mr. Herzinger

We are sitting in Carlotta's mother's walk-in closet, her shoes tossed around us on the lower shelves. We didn't make this mess. This is how Carlotta's mother, Kim, keeps her things, strewn around like scraps of old wrapping paper. Carlotta has a gypsy scarf tied around her forehead. The long part keeps falling down across her face when Carlotta examines my palm, and she has to push it back over her hair. I am not sure how a gypsy wears a scarf, but I know that Carlotta has got it wrong.

"You will have seven, no, eight children," she says to me, flipping up the scarf. Then she looks into my eyes. "One may be weird," she says, "even retarded."

Outside in Kim's bedroom our mothers are talking, sitting in light pink chaise lounges by the window. Sometimes we hear them laugh, Kim's giggle or my mother's donkey laugh. Whenever my mother laughs, Carlotta and I cover our mouths like we could die. That's what my mother's laugh makes us do.

My baby brother Charlie pulls open the closet door and smiles his drooly smile at us. My mother comes up behind him, grabs him around the middle, and carries him back to the window where they have set out his toys.

"You forgot to shut the door," I yell at my mom, pushing it closed.

"You girls better not be making a mess in there," Kim yells.

"Please, Mom," Carlotta yells. "Can't we have a little peace?"

There are other rooms that we could be playing in, Carlotta's room for one, but we are here instead because the Herzingers' bedroom is where things happen in this house, where our mothers talk, and where some nights the exotic Mr. Herzinger comes home to sleep.

Mr. Herzinger's things are not in this closet. He has his own closet. All of the clothes in it are ironed, hung at the creases. He keeps his shoes in plastic bags, each pair zipped in, airtight. He comes home for a few days each month, to air out his shoes, Carlotta says.

*

I have heard this retarded baby story before, and even though it doesn't scare me anymore, I make my hand tremble a little as Carlotta picks it up and looks into it again.

"The baby will have wings when it's born," she says, leaning down so close, I feel her eyelashes flicker across my palm. "But don't worry, they'll fall off before he learns to fly."

Outside the closet our mothers are talking softly now, too softly to hear much of anything so I crack open the closet door, and Carlotta and I sit close together and listen.

"Men should be leashed as soon as they learn to walk," Kim says.

I peek out the crack, Carlotta leaning over my shoulder. Kim is holding up her pink sweatshirt and pulling out the thick elastic of her bra, showing my mom a bruise under her breast, the bruise the size of a large thumb-print, dark enough for me to see from here. My mom reaches out to touch it, and I push the door closed shut so Carlotta cannot see anymore. "Sick," I hear my mother say. No matter how much my parents fight, there is never anything as real as this bruise to show for it. I put a pair of Kim's shoes on my hands and walk them up the shelves to distract and entertain Carlotta. These are some of my favorites, shiny black, edged with jewels, rhinestones running down the back, even a red, red ruby chipped open at the outside of the heel.

"Sleep over tonight," Carlotta says. "Please. You know your mother will say yes. We don't have school tomorrow, do we?"

"It's Saturday," I say, "no school tomorrow." This is Carlotta's weakness, days of the week, remembering the order, how many are left in the weekend, before school's out for summer, even before her birthday. Because I have seen Kim's bruise, I don't pick on Carlotta when I tell her what day it is.

"We can both sleep in my bed," Carlotta says. "I won't make you sleep in the trundle."

"Come here you," I hear my mother say. Then, "What a big boy." She unzips her purse, and Carlotta and I both listen to the sound of her nail clippers, the efficient metal snaps as they move—one, two, three, four, five—across the fingernails on each of Charlie's hands, across all ten toenails.

*

In Mr. Herzinger's study there is a model of a Ferris wheel. All of the seats are painted different colors—orange, green, yellow, pink, white—stranger colors, too. Carlotta calls one charuse, another maude. She taps a Ferris-wheel chair with her finger and lets it spin. Every single part of the Ferris wheel works just a like a real one. When we crank it up it plays "Take Me Out to the Ball Game."

Lining the walls of Mr. Herzinger's study are photographs of Ferris wheels, all bright and new, with Mr. Herzinger the only person on each, riding way up at the top, one hand high in the air, waving.

While we are playing in Mr. Herzinger's study, my mom and Kim are in the kitchen feeding Charlie and making us dinner. Soon my mother will go home, and I'll stay and wear one of Carlotta's silky nightgowns all around the house for hours before it's time to go to sleep.

My mother and I have both been lonely since my mother's boyfriend, Bill, who I never really liked that much, left for Florida two months ago. I am lonely because now my mother is sad most of the time, because it is only with Kim, not me, that she laughs these days.

Although it's already May, we aren't ready for summer yet, our bathing suits still packed away in the garage.

My father, who doesn't—I don't think—exactly know about Bill, seems to know that something is different and tried to cheer my mother and me up at first, telling jokes, once bringing home two gerbils in a fish tank filled with wood chips. I told my father that the gerbils escaped because Charlie wouldn't keep the wire-mesh lid on top of the cage. But the truth is that when Myrtle, our babysitter, said she couldn't think right with all of that racket the gerbils made in the corner of the den, like drilling in the street, my mother and I took the gerbils to the beach and let them go by the ocean. My mother said that they could either drown or run from the waves, that was their choice, but it wasn't worth losing Myrtle to domesticated rodents.

*

My mother kisses me on the forehead, holding my head between her hands while Carlotta and I are eating dinner. She tells me to be good and to come home early in the morning, not to overstay my welcome. She holds my brother Charlie out to me, and I shake his feet in my hands. He is still so young that every part of him is pretty, even his feet. I am almost ten and have not let anyone touch my feet for years.

"Where's your dad?" I ask Carlotta while her mother walks my mother to the door.

Carlotta shrugs. "He was here yesterday. I think he went to Tokyo. My mom and I are going to visit Craig tomorrow, you know. That's why you have to go home early."

Craig is Carlotta's older brother. He lives at the Children's Seashore Home in Atlantic City. He's sixteen and still sucks his thumb. I see him during the summers when Kim drives him home to visit, Carlotta sitting in the front seat between them, Craig's toys thrown around in the bed of the station wagon, his head hanging out the window, his mouth open to the wind.

"My father won't come with us ever anymore," Carlotta says to me and drinks her milk. "That's one of the things they fight about these days."

After dinner we take our baths and are clean and damp, standing in our underpants in Kim's closet. Kim is spraying us with perfume, puffing clouds of sweet-smelling powder under our arms. Everything is different at this house. Sometimes I am an angel, sometimes a goddess of love.

"You girls are devastating tonight," Kim says to us and sneezes from so much talc.

My mother, who is younger and wears less makeup than Kim, has no perfumes, only small tubes of oil that she keeps in the medicine cabinet. Sometimes she dabs me with civet or rose behind the knees. But with Kim, we are lavished with scents. She drapes fake furs over our shoulders. We parade this way around the house, taking turns being Miss America and her runner-up, throwing kisses to our fans.

We are finally so worn-out from our hot baths and the dress-ups that Carlotta and I collapse on the Herzingers' bed. Kim sits on a chaise lounge that she has turned to face us. She looks tired, hair clips loose and strands of thin, blond-white hair hanging straight at her shoulders.

*

Before Craig was born, Mr. Herzinger and Kim didn't live in Avalon. They lived everywhere Mr. Herzinger went to build a new Ferris wheel. I've seen pictures from then. Kim and Mr. Herzinger looked like movie stars, their hair oiled-down in the sun. I cannot imagine my parents ever having traveled together that way, in love, eating foreign foods, speaking other languages. My father works at an office all day in Atlantic City. Even when they are fighting, my parents yell at each other from different rooms, sometimes separate floors. They seem like they hardly know each other. My mother says that seventeen was too young to get married.

I have known Kim and Carlotta my whole life, but I don't remember much about the beginning. Sometimes Kim and my mother tell us stories about when we were babies or about the summer when they were pregnant with us and first became friends. Boys used to drive by and whistle on their way to the beach before they saw our mothers' bellies, round over their shorts, reflected in the their rearview mirrors. Our mothers talk about those times and they laugh.

On Memorial Day, when the rides open for the summer on the Wildwood Boardwalk, I always get my mom to take Carlotta and me. The first thing you see when you look out at the piers is Mr. Herzinger's Ferris wheel. It takes my breath away each time, but Carlotta shrugs and buys some cotton candy, makes me wait in line with her to get on the roller coaster.

*

Kim stretches out her legs on the chaise lounge and closes her eyes. Carlotta is falling asleep next to me. Very quietly I get up and pull down the sheet a little like my mother does for me while I'm brushing my teeth at night. I wake Carlotta and we get under the covers while Kim sleeps on the chaise lounge, our skin warm and clean on the sheets, our hair across her pillows.

I wake up once during the night and find Kim has gotten into bed and is sleeping on the other side of me. I can feel someone else in the room, someone watching us. For a second I think it's Craig, big and sad, crying quietly in the corner. But when I look up, it's the exotic Mr. Herzinger himself I see standing in the doorway, his hand up high in the air, telling me hello, or maybe saying goodbye, waving at me when I smile at him this way, deep in the damp of their bed.

Naked Lake

I want to explain how it happened that I saw the woman who lives next door while she was naked. Jimmy, Curtis, and Gail were sitting out back on the deck talking about how they wanted to quit their jobs and try something new. My husband, Jimmy, he's the one who started the conversation. He likes to get people going. Gail's been a secretary for as long as I've known her, and I doubt that she has the confidence required to ever find anything else. And Curtis, although he used to answer almost any kind of want ad, he wouldn't risk their financial security by quitting his computer job now that he and Gail are married. I was the only one who wasn't talking much. Me, I tend to be cynical these days about a lot of talk that comes to nothing, and believe me, I'd heard this kind of talk before.

The woman next door was in her house, upstairs in the bathroom with the light on, the curtain open, and the window closed. I don't suspect that she knew we were even out there, that she was putting on a show for anyone. She was just standing in a calm, yellow light, washing herself by the sink in this real slow, precise way—under her arms, moving her light blue washcloth in smooth circles.

Jimmy was saying he might as well just quit and do nothing at all, that I could support the both of us with the new raise I just got. "Hell," he said, "I may as well just take it easy for a while, just sit back and let myself be a kept man."

Although I do make decent money updating mailing lists for the American Engineering Association, it's nothing two people could live on. My job is just a job, but Jimmy actually likes his work. He makes videotapes of weddings, bar mitzvahs, fiftieth-anniversary parties, and he makes videos of more solemn events, too—swearing-ins and even funerals, on occasion. Once in a while, even though I have my own job now, if he has an event to shoot on the weekend, I still go with him, help with the audio and watch him there behind his camera, tall and in charge, his blond hair tapered to a V at the back of his neck. I watch him make decisions about angles, about what to include and what to leave out, in charge of how the whole thing will be remembered. The final product.

Curtis said, "Nothing at all? I don't know what I'd do with myself all day if I didn't work. Watch television, I guess. Maybe take up some kind of depressing hobby like coin collecting."

Gail sighed when she heard that one. Ever since Gail found out she can't conceive, she's been doing a lot of sighing. Gail crossed her legs, and as her feet flashed out in front of me for an instant, I could see that, as always, the little squared-off pads on the heels of her shoes were new and spongy. "I wouldn't be bored for at least a year," she said. "I'd write letters to everyone I owe letters to, and I might take a class. Maybe some kind of craft class. Something I've never tried before like calligraphy or making jewelry. I've always been good with my hands."

Jimmy and Curtis both smiled at that one, smiled at my expense, I might add. Although she's married to Curtis now, Gail had once dated Jimmy, too. And normally I would have minded their smiles and would have minded even more the way Gail looked down instead of getting angry after she realized that she had made a joke, but my eyes went straight up instead, up to the lady who was washing herself in the upstairs bathroom next door. What she was doing was lifting up a small breast and softly rubbing her damp washcloth under it. I don't think I'd ever seen anything that pretty before, and I wanted to tap Jimmy—who was sitting across from me—on the foot, to get him to look up too, but you never know what Jimmy's reaction to something is going to be. Maybe he'd be real quiet about it, and later after Curtis and Gail went home, we'd both imagine that woman next door while we were getting undressed for bed. Maybe, though, he'd make a big deal out of it, elbow Curtis in the side so he'd look up too, and before you knew it, the whole thing would be ruined, changed into something ugly. So I kept the woman next door to myself. Whenever the conversation got boring, I'd glance right up at her.

I'd seen this woman plenty of times with clothes on, and I'd never thought much of her. She seemed to me like a quick-shower kind of person, efficient and brisk, very different than me. (Even during the hottest part of the summer, I like to lower myself slowly into a bathtub full of water so hot that it pains me as I watch the skin on my feet turn from flesh-color to pink.) With clothes on, she's too skinny and she has this overbite that might look kind of childish and attractive on some women, but on her those teeth look as if they're trying to escape her mouth. I've never seen any husband or boyfriend with her, and I figure it's her skinniness and overbite or maybe just her plain mean nature that drove her children's father away.

The thing about her is that she's mean to her kids. She yanks them by the arms when they can't keep up with her, and I've seen her play this spooky game with the little one when they're out in their yard taking the clothes off the line. She positions herself in such a way that the wind sticks a shirt to her face, and she leaves it there, making all kinds of low, angry noises despite the fact that her kid is protesting the whole time, saying things like *Mommy, I'm scared. Let me see you.*

Gail said, "No, seriously. I always got As in art all the way through the twelfth grade. I used to draw these little scenes, so small they'd fit right on the bottom of a dessert plate. In fact, that's how I started out, my mother says. She'd buy paper dessert plates for me at the grocery store, and I'd turn them over and color right on them."

I could imagine Gail doing this, drawing real small scenes. Gail is petite and careful. Before she sits down, she brushes the seat off first with the side of her hand even if the seat is already clean. Whenever she's around, I watch Jimmy to see if he notices how my fingernail polish has begun to chip around the tips of my fingernails, how my sweater could use a dry-cleaning.

"What kinds of things did you draw?" I asked.

"Well, when I was little, all the regular things—houses, flowers, a nice, pretty family all holding hands together. But later I got into biblical scenes. I drew this real tiny Virgin Mary and the little baby Jesus in the manger, and then I painted everything in, even the hay in the manger, and the little baby Jesus. I got even his toenails looking like the real thing, my art teacher said."

Except for the sound of Gail sighing, it was kind of quiet after that, probably because everyone was thinking what I was thinking, about the little baby Jesus and how Gail could never have a baby. Even if she were able to manage some kind of immaculate conception, her womb wouldn't work right. I watched Curtis run his fingers back through his hair, exposing his receding hairline and a pockmark left from when he had the chicken pox. I wanted to look up then at the lady next door, but this was the wrong moment, I knew. Everyone would follow my eyes right up there, grateful for any kind of distraction.

"How about another joint?" Jimmy said. Jimmy always did have good timing at social occasions. Sometimes when I'm trying to think about all of the good things about him so I can remember why I fell in love with him, I light on his perfect social timing.

"Is this, or is this not, supreme marijuana," Jimmy said, passing it to Gail—guests first, ladies first—even though Gail never smokes and passed it right on to Curtis.

The conversation switched over to crime, where it was safe to live these days, and everyone got really interested in that. Even Gail's mood picked up a little. "I hear that Washington State is a nice place," she said. "Green and pretty and not too many people." And then Curtis disagreed with her. He started getting really animated, talking about how all of the mass murderers go up to Tacoma to prey on the innocent and unsuspecting. Curtis had all kinds of murder stories stored away in his mind—names, dates, how each killing was performed. It was kind of interesting, but, still, I didn't much like hearing about it.

I looked up at her bathroom window again. I figured she'd be done by now, but she was still there. From the way she was bent over and the movement of her arm, I could see that she was shaving one of her legs, had lifted that leg right up onto the rim of the sink and was balancing on the other leg. I could see the bones arching across her back, her breast not quite touching her knee, her gray-brown nipples pointing down, her face all concentrated and intent.

Now don't get me wrong. I've seen plenty of women naked before, and I don't mean just family members and friends either. Before we got married, Jimmy and I used to go to this pond we found in the mountains. We called the pond Naked Lake, although its real name was something like Schooner's Landing. Jimmy and I would take off our clothes in the car and run naked through the woods. When we reached the pond, we would dive right in without even toe-touching the water first, without even looking around us. When we came up in the water, we'd see all the other naked people sunbathing and playing Frisbee by the edge of the water. Sometimes, even before we surfaced, I'd open my eyes under water and see a naked person gliding right past me.

I must have been a little stoned by this point or I never would have interrupted Curtis and said what I said. "Jimmy," I said, "how come we don't ever go to Naked Lake anymore?"

Everyone looked at me, surprised to hear me interrupt. "Naked Lake?" Curtis said. "Shit, girl. I've lived here my whole life, and I never heard of any Naked Lake. What all have you been keeping from me?"

"That's just some place we went on our honeymoon," Jimmy said.

"In Bermuda. Lee's got everything confused. She's had too much to smoke."

"Never mind," I said, even though Jimmy lied about Naked Lake. It's just three hours away, and we didn't go there on our honeymoon. But I didn't say anything about Jimmy lying, not that he would have done anything to stop me if I did go on because, as I said, he's nothing if not polite when it comes to social occasions.

After that, Gail looked at her watch and said that since they still had jobs and a mortgage, they'd better get going so they could make it in to work on time the next day.

"The voice of reason and cruel reality," Curtis said, but you could tell that he was just teasing her. He took one last hit and put the joint out in the ashtray.

"How about having some cake first?" I said. "I completely forgot to bring out the cake."

Curtis looked at Gail and she said, "No, you all can have it later. We really have to be going."

"It's a lemon cake, with icing, the kind you like," I said to Curtis.

"Thanks anyway, Lee," Curtis said. He patted his stomach. "But I've got to keep an eye on the old weight."

Jimmy and I both walked them to the front door and watched them get into their car. As I stood there next to Jimmy watching them, I felt the cramp set in down at the small of my back and begin to work its way up to the base of my neck. I began searching my head for some reason to call them back. When I finally thought about shouting to Gail that I forgot to show her a new skirt I bought, when I finally thought of yelling to her that she had to come have a look at this skirt and use her artistic sense to tell me what blouse would work with it, it was too late. Gail had flipped on the interior light, pulled down her windshield visor and was already checking her face in the mirror, smoothing out a thin eyebrow, and Curtis was revving up the engine of their car. I walked with Jimmy back inside the house and shut the door.

For a while neither of us said anything, but I knew that now that we were alone together, all of the rules were different. I walked through the house and started picking up beer cans from the deck and carrying them into the kitchen. When I was bent down over the garbage can, I felt Jimmy standing behind me. I stayed down there for a while, rearranging the garbage at the top of the can, pushing air out of the empty bag of chips to make room for the beer cans. I bent the cans in half, making them smaller, stacking them up one on top of the other, listening to Jimmy breathing behind me. I had this idea that if I stayed in one place and held my breath in, if I just stayed still and listened to Jimmy's body behind me, the blood working its way steadily through it, I could figure out his mood. I finally let the air out of my lungs and stood up when I felt Jimmy's fingers close in lightly around the bones of my hips in a way that was familiar, in a way that meant that everything would be all right for now.

"Hey, let's not ruin everything tonight," he said. "We'll just pretend that didn't happen."

I turned around and looked at him. No matter how many times I tried not to, I still turned right around and looked at him.

"Come here," I said. "I want to show you something." I took his hand and led him out back.

"Look." I pointed up at her bathroom window. This time I knew for certain that she'd still be there. She had her head bent down, and she was brushing her hair out over her face. Even her hair, which is thin and bleached-pale during the rest of the day, looked pretty and glowing up there in the yellow light.

"Damn," Jimmy said.

We just stood there together, watching her for a long time. Jimmy, I knew, was in a kind of trance, the way I had been, and I didn't want to let him know what I was thinking. I was thinking about that time at Naked Lake, the last time we went there, right before we got married, how Jimmy promised me that it would never happen again. He had smacked me up against his car that day because he thought I had flirted with the man who whistled at me as we walked past.

And me, I was younger then. I said to Jimmy that day, *I love you, I believe you.*

Honeymoon

Our motel pool in Anaheim is full of Farm Families of America: pale, fleshy women wearing skirted bathing suits, their vaguely startled-looking husbands and overeager, corn-fed children are floating everywhere. The women are mostly gathered around the perimeter, talking about God-knows-what. From my lounge chair, I catch a few choice words: *cross-stitch, soybeans, solar eclipse, grandbaby*.

While the Farm Families of America have their convention, my husband of two weeks sleeps in the lounge chair beside me, dreaming, no doubt, of Space Mountain, the final frontier of our amusement-theme-park-themed honeymoon, which we plan to conquer tomorrow. Yes, he is young enough to be my son, but only if I had him at a ridiculously young age. Sleep is his way of dealing with strife, and, frankly, I'm hoping he outgrows this particular coping mechanism and replaces it with a more mature one, such as having a vodka tonic or maybe a long, hot soak in the tub.

I slowly get up, a little more careful than usual to make sure my body is tucked into my bathing suit, and take my drink over to the hot tub, which appears to be a Farm Family–free zone. The only people in it, a tanned couple wearing matching Mickey Mouse–insignia tennis visors and holding beak-shaped Styrofoam beer can holders, barely seem to notice me slip in and sit across from them. I take note of her thick-knuckled hand—complete with large but foggy diamond and wedding band—gripping her beer holder, his failure to shave that morning, and decide I know their type: holiday hedonists, who view playing a round of tennis and then sitting in a hot tub with a cheap, cold beer as their idea of nirvana. That is, the kind of couple too immersed in their own good fortune to strike up a conversation with a stranger. Me, for example.

From my new vantage point in the hot tub, I have both a better and worse view of the Farm Families. As I'm on their level now, so to speak, when one of them decides to get out of the pool, I can see first his face, followed by sloping shoulders, meaty chest, and so on as he ascends the underwater ladder, as opposed to seeing them each in total from the relative on-high position of my lounge chair. My husband seems to still be asleep, but he could just be faking it. In fact, he could have been faking it all along, his coping mechanism even more childish than I had thought: pretending to sleep to avoid strife.

Just as I begin to relax, the hot tub stops bubbling, and I suddenly have a clear underwater view of my neighbors. He's wearing a high-waisted Speedo, which, as with most men's attire, could signal anything from severe poor taste to a misguided concern with comfort above fashion. Her bathing suit causes me more immediate alarm. While not skirted, it is plain navy blue with a higher than average neckline and a little girl sailor anchor above the chest. I begin to worry she's going to try to engage me in a conversation about canning preserves but decide I'm wrong when she opens her eyes and takes a swig of beer.

"The thing is you have to get out to push the button," she says to me. "If you want more bubbles, that is. I'm not sure I'm up to the challenge."

Just when I'm about to offer a noncommittal smile of agreement, a beach ball is flung into the water, first grazing the top of my head, and even her husband, who I am also beginning to suspect of faking sleep, finally opens his eyes and says, "What the fuck?"

"Whoopsie daisy," a freckled-kneed teenage girl says, splashing in after it. "Ouch. How do you guys take this?" she asks.

"With a twist of lime, preferably," Ms. Hot Tub says and smiles at me conspiratorially.

"Whatever," Miss Farm Families teenager says, high-stepping it out of there before her doughy calves turn red.

I close my eyes, hoping to avoid full-fledged conversation. Don't get me wrong. I am not, as a rule, an unfriendly person. What I am, after two weeks of honeymooning at amusement parks with Graham, is good and ready to get back home.

When Mr. and Ms. Hot Tub begin to argue about whose turn it is to reset the bubbles, I take this as my cue to get out myself, and as a parting gesture of goodwill, hit the button for them before heading back to Graham. He's still asleep or at least still pretending to sleep, his mouth slightly open, his arms limp at his sides. All at once I decide *Damn the Farm Families* and sit down on top of him, straddle-style, tapping the pads of my fingers lightly on his chest. "It's raining, it's pouring," I say. "Graham is getting boring." I watch him fight off a smile, shy-boy style, and dare any woman here not to envy me.

"Have you reconsidered?" he asks, not opening his eyes.

"Jesus. Are we still on that?" I say, tapping just a little too hard now like I'm typing on a manual.

He opens his eyes, takes hold of my wrists, and pushes my hands off him.

"Okay, if it's a boy, we'll have him circumcised," I say, referring to the future child that Graham just yesterday decided he wanted in his annoyingly young, whimsical style as we waited in line to buy our tickets at Knott's Berry Farm, never once stopping to consider that my eggs have all been completely accounted for by now.

"Congratulations, you two," I hear a vaguely familiar voice say, and see Ms. Hot Tub plop herself down in the lounge chair next to us, her Styrofoam beer holder in hand, condiments and the remnants of an earlier poolside feast at the end of the chair by her feet.

I signal the poolside waiter and order another vodka tonic, waiting for Ms. Hot Tub to raise her eyebrows at me for drinking while pregnant, but instead she goes right on.

"Me, I was never blessed in that way. With any children, that is. Not that there aren't other ways of being blessed, which I certainly am, many times over. This morning, for example, I was blessed with a truly excellent backhand. Isn't that right, Vic?" she says to her husband, who I now see is lying down on his belly in the chair next to her.

"Are you planning to use that mustard?" Graham says, raising the back of his chair up now, and pushing me off to the side, so I'm now facing Ms. Hot Tub instead of my new husband.

"I collect them. Souvenirs," he says, picking up the dwarfed bottle that came with her poolside sandwich before she has a chance to answer him. It's true. Our suitcase is full of them. We have room service–sized bottles from six not quite first-rate southern California hotels.

"I guess not," she says, looking not at all certain.

"Excellent," Graham says, "because I don't believe I have this bottle yet, and it would be a super addition to my collection."

This is the way my husband of two weeks talks. Excellent. Super. Just then, a string-filled rendition of "The Age of Aquarius" begins to be piped in through speakers I hadn't noticed before, and I am filled with bleakness. To cheer myself up, I decide to shock Ms. Beer-Drinking Hot Tub, who appears to be about my age, although, as is the case with most women my age, not nearly so well kept-up. "I performed in a production of *Hair*," I say. "I was Donna, the sixteen-year-old virgin who finally gets laid."

"Sex can be a beautiful thing when two people love each other. Isn't that right, Vic?" He grunts his approval, and I realize the completeness of my mistake. They are not the kind of people too immersed in their own happiness to bother with me. They are instead, or at least she is, the kind of vacationers who consider meeting new folks the best part of any trip. In other words, the kind that are hardest to shake. I say, "Okay, I'm turning in. Ready, Graham, honey?"

"How do you feel about baptism?" he asks. "Because I'm starting to lean that way myself."

"Absolutely," Ms. Hot Tub says. "Why not hedge your bets?"

Three Farm Families of America children gallop by us, pretending to be horses, while Ms. Hot Tub and my husband discuss whether Disneyland can really be seen in one visit. I can tell Graham is being convinced at this moment that Frontierland alone is worthy of its own day. The waiter appears with my drink, and because Graham is deep in conversation, I sign for it myself, using my first name and Graham's last, feeling as if I'm forging someone else's signature.

I take my drink and stand up, making a point of patting my very firm, thank you, belly. "We're getting hungry," I say and grab my purse and begin walking away, knowing Graham will eventually fall behind me.

"Nice meeting you," I hear but pretend not to. I stop at the ice machine and look back at the pool where the corn-fed children are hitting the beach ball up in the air in a makeshift game of volleyball. I hide next to the far side of the ice machine and watch Graham stop talking and survey the area, looking for unopened mustard bottles. When he's satisfied he hasn't missed any, he pulls on his Magic Mountain T-shirt and comes looking for me. My husband of two weeks nears the ice machine, full of its noisy rumblings.

"Caught me," I say, stepping out in front of him. I feel the ground cool under my feet as I step on Graham's shadow.

"Cool," Graham's says. "Now we can ride down together."

The skin on my face feels tight from the sun, so to avoid being caught looking deficient in the unflattering light of the elevator, I look down instead of at Graham, bend over and pretend to examine a freckle on my calf. And for the first time I notice something that I have not noticed in the entire two weeks we have been married. My husband of two weeks is missing half a toe. From the fourth toe, to be specific, right foot.

Before I can ask him about it and what else he's hiding from me, we're in the lobby, and, still in my bathing suit, I'm following Graham to the coffee shop. Despite the wealth of empty tables we pass, he allows us to be seated in a remote corner under the ventilation system where the most novice waiter is certainly stationed. During the first week of our honeymoon, Graham sat next to me in restaurants, despite the fact that our elbows banged when we cut our food. The only future we talked about was how far we wanted to drive the next day.

Our waiter wears a round pin next to his name—Zachary—that reads: *Please be Patient—I'm New!* Before taking our drink orders, Zachary gives a worried look in the direction of the poolside mustard bottle Graham has set out on the table to admire.

A fully dressed Farm Family follows the hostess to a table near us. It's a better spot, less remote, under a huge fake fern instead of the ventilation system. A real waitress takes their order, and before our waiter can even manage to bring us water, I watch them sip theirs and then *ooh* over the slices of lemon floating in their lemonades.

When the Farm Family's food arrives, they hold hands and lower their heads. "Your turn, honey," the dad says and gives his daughter's hand a few quick pulsing squeezes.

"Thank you, Lord, for the meal we're about to eat and for making Daddy's convention be in Disneyland this year instead of Topeka like it was last year and for giving us enough fun money to spend so we could all come. Amen."

"Amen," they all say and then their silverware begins clanging.

I kick Graham under the table, but he misunderstands and catches my foot between his calves and holds it there, which, in fact, I don't mind at all. Zachary brings our food before our water, but I'm too hungry to complain.

"I don't care how long the line is this afternoon, we're not leaving here without doing Pirates of the Caribbean," Graham says, my foot still caught between his calves, all of my fully intact toes sliding their way up to his knees. "I couldn't stand it if you had to tell our grandchildren you missed that one." He finishes admiring his mustard bottle and hands it to me to put in my purse.

When we leave, the Farm Family has just begun to work their way through dessert, a huge dollop of whipped cream on top of each of their slices of pie. I follow Graham past their table, watch the way my husband's body moves under his Magic Mountain T-shirt and swim trunks. At first I don't recognize Mr. and Mrs. Hot Tub in their matching blue shorts and white shirts when they wave us over to them in the lobby. No one but Graham and I are in our bathing suits down here.

"You two absolutely have to sit with us at the fireworks tonight," Mrs. Hot Tub says to Graham. She opens a flat gray gift-shop bag and takes out a postcard. Leaning on her husband's back, she draws Graham a diagram on the reverse side of a lurid-looking sunset. "I'm saving you both a place right next to us. You have to get there early, you know, to get a good spot."

"I'd love to stay and chat, but we have to go have sex right now," I tell her. "It's our honeymoon. It's required."

Graham shrugs a suddenly very husband-like what-am-I-going-to-do-with-her shrug and takes the postcard from her. He opens my purse and drops it in next to the mustard bottle. "Excellent," he says. "See you there."

In the elevator, I look down at the place where my husband of two weeks is missing part of his toe, at the way it's been clipped off right above the knuckle. "Birth defect?" I whisper, as we step off the elevator and head back to our room to change into our clothes, but Graham doesn't hear me. Why would he? He's too busy thinking about the future again. An extra day at Disneyland, then *cross-stitch, grandbaby*. You can hear it in the way he walks now, the key to our room already out, his steps full of inexhaustible purpose.

The Visit

My mother's earrings have taken over the bathroom. They are everywhere—twisted silver threads, heavy wedged triangles, loose oval hoops. My daughter, Jamie, stands on tiptoe each morning when she is finished brushing her teeth and matches her grandmother's earrings into pairs, hooks each pair together by their thin wires, and lines them up next to each other in the lid of the box her pink ballet shoes came in, a box she gives all indication of having saved for this very purpose.

My mother has been camping out in the backyard for the past two weeks. When Sophie arrived for her visit with the tent and sleeping bag, my husband, Frank, said, "To each his own," and helped her drive in the stakes. Frank had only been back for a week himself, and I knew he was trying not to make any more trouble. As for me, I couldn't say what felt odder the next morning, waking up and seeing my mother's tent in the backyard, or looking from the window back over to the bed I had become used to sleeping in alone, and finding Frank there.

It's not as if I didn't invite Sophie to stay in the house. I pressed clean sheets and handed her the extra key, but now that Frank had come back, Sophie wouldn't hear of it. "Nothing beats the earth for a pillow," she said, "and, besides, the idea was that I was coming here for a vacation, not to put any of you out."

Each night after we've all done the dinner dishes, Jamie and I walk my mother across the lawn so Jamie can kiss her grandmother good night. After Jamie is tucked in upstairs, I walk back downstairs, turn out the living room lights, and stare out at the bright spot in the back-yard. Sometimes I make myself a drink, and while I wait for my mother's flashlight to blink out, I listen to Frank in the basement below me, working on some project he's left half complete for years. Now that he's back he says that he's going to finish them all up for me, but the truth is I don't even know what's down there anymore.

When it gets quiet in the basement this usually means that Frank will be heading up the stairs after a while with his tape measure, stretching it out across a section of the living room wall. "You're go-ing to love this," is what he always says to me as he jots down the numbers on a pad of paper. It's easier for him to talk to me now when he's busy doing something else and doesn't have to look up. I don't mind: it's easier for me, too. It bothers me less for him to avoid my eyes and concentrate on something else than for him to stare straight at me.

Each night as I fall asleep, I imagine my mother slapping at the mosquitoes she's zipped inside her tent.

*

This morning Frank got up before me, opened the blinds, looked out our bedroom window and shook his head at my mother's tent. "Looks like the crazy lady's still here," he said. I wanted to tell him to stop talking about my mother that way, but I didn't say anything. Ever since Frank's come back, I've been careful about what I say to him. Even little arguments seem to belong to what I've come to think of as our previous life, the life we had before Frank went away.

Besides, it wouldn't have been any use arguing with him—Frank's not the only one talking anymore. The neighbors on both sides are beginning to make comments. After work Louise, to the right, catches up with me at the Safeway, in Mexican Foods. "What do you think? With garlic and peppers or not?" she says, holding up a can of refried beans in each hand.

Knowing Louise well enough to know that she's not really interested in my advice, I say, "With. Always with. They're much better that way," thinking that this is the kind of definitive statement that will end our conversation quickly.

Caught off-guard, Louise places both cans in her empty cart. "I see your mother's still communing with nature," she says, reading over the ingredients on a box of taco shells now.

"Would you look at the time?" I say. "I'm going to be late for picking up Jamie at ballet class." And with that I wheel my cart away to the checkout, forgetting all about the rest of my list until later that night when Jamie and I are getting ready to bake a spice cake for her elementary school's bake sale, and I find that I'm still out of nutmeg.

Knowing Louise the way I do, I write off her nosiness as simply annoying, but Jerome's the one who really gets me thinking. The whole time I've lived next door to him, he's only spoken to me on occasions of absolute seriousness, like the time he hurt his back shoveling snow and wanted to know if I had a couple of Advils he could try for it. And even then, he knocked so lightly on my side door that the only reason I heard him at all was because I happened to be sitting in that chair by the door, still trying to work out the Sunday crossword.

So yesterday when Jerome made a point of walking out to the road to pick up his mail at the *exact* same time I picked up mine, I knew that he'd been watching for me from his kitchen window and had something to say about it.

"Good morning, Jerome," I said to him as a truck rushed by and I reached into my mailbox. "How's that back of yours doing now that the weather's warmer? Are they going to let you go back to work soon?" I smiled up at him like there was nothing unusual about the two of us running into each other this way.

Jerome rested one hand against his lower back as if I had made it start hurting again by just mentioning it, and held onto his mail with the other. "Nah," he said. "Says I got to take it easy for at least another month."

"Well, that's not so much longer," I said.

"Megan," he said, squaring the envelopes in his hand, "I was wondering about that tent in your backyard."

"Oh, that," I said. "Nothing to wonder about. It's just my mother, trying to stay out of everyone's way."

"Your mother's sleeping in a tent?" he said.

"Sure is," I said as if I were proud of her.

"Well, I guess as long as it isn't kids up to trouble," he said, "there's no harm in it."

"No harm at all," I said. "Just an older lady taking in the fresh air."

"Sleeps on the ground, does she?" Jerome said.

"Foam pad."

"Hey to Frank then," Jerome said, nodding at Frank's car in the driveway and frowning to let me know he was still uneasy about the situation, before walking back up the driveway to his house.

*

The truth is that getting close to nature seems to be the furthest thing from my mother's mind. Sophie's piled up three foam pads on which to rest her sleeping bag. She's purchased a used, industrial-sized radio that picks up two television stations and even a radio station from as far away as Norfolk. It's Sunday afternoon, and Frank and Jamie are at a baseball game when I finally get up the nerve to go out and talk to my mother about how much longer she plans to camp out.

During the past two weeks I have carefully avoided the problem of how to announce myself at Sophie's tent by sending Jamie out in the yard ahead of me, yelling for her grandmother. But today Jamie is gone, and, at a loss, I first try knocking lightly on the cloth. When I get no reaction, I clear my throat and say, "Mom, can I come in?" Sophie yells for me to unzip the entrance myself because her nail polish is still drying.

"Shh," she says to me as I pull my knees up to my chest, trying to make myself comfortable in a corner of my mother's tent. "I want to get this phone number down right." So she doesn't ruin her nail polish, Sophie balances a pen between the inside of her thumb and her ring finger, like someone who's mastered the wrong instructions on how to use chop sticks, as she leans down and writes the phone number from the radio onto a pad of paper.

"A camp stove complete with a new fuel tank," she says, shaking her head, "and they're only asking fifteen. Imagine."

"Who, Mother?" I say, already feeling my legs begin to cramp at the back of my knees.

"I didn't get the last name. Someone named Irving. Irving something," she says.

On the radio now is Frieda who wants fifty dollars for her good-as-new air-conditioning window unit complete with a new air filter and forty dollars for her chainsaw with the spark-arrester. Sophie creases the skin above her nose to alert me that she is listening intently and I shouldn't interrupt, holds her fingers out in front of her and blows on her nails.

"Mother," I say, "we've got to talk."

"She's hard up for money," Sophie says, shaking her head at the radio. "No other reason to sell a perfectly good window unit."

"Maybe she got central put in," I say.

"I don't think so," Sophie says. "If she could afford central, she could afford to give the unit away to her kids."

"Maybe she doesn't have kids," I say, trying to poke holes in my mother's argument—an old habit that seems childish to me even as I give into it.

"Well, she's got somebody," Sophie says. "Everybody's got *somebody*."

"Maybe she's moving somewhere where it doesn't get hot the way it does here," I say, "and she needs the money to get resettled."

"Like I said. She's hard up for cash."

"Fine, Mother," I say, finally giving in. "You win, okay."

"If I win then you have to take me to get the camp stove."

"Okay," I say, relieved that our talk would be postponed for few minutes, despite my resolve to confront my mother.

But, of course, our talk is postponed for longer than that. Sophie goes inside to call Irving and get his address, and when we finally get in the car, she spreads out the map on her lap and insists on directing me to his house. For nearly twenty years my mother worked for a moving company in Baltimore, and she still prides herself in knowing how to read a map quickly and efficiently.

When my father left and Sophie first started working, she treated her new job as if it were something gravely important, at least as important as my father's departure. The afternoon Sophie drove up to the school bus stop and motioned for me to get in the car, she told me about both these things. "Your father still loves you but he's going to love you from somewhere else from now on," she said, "and your mother has a job."

It was less a surprise to me that my father had left than that Sophie had gotten a job. My father often left for days at a time on business trips. When he came back he'd call me into the living room and ask me the kind of questions adults I hardly knew asked, a safe, boring category of school questions—Are you looking forward to the second grade? Do you have homework yet? During these sessions with him I felt watched in a way that made me want to pronounce every word carefully and correctly, and when Sophie told me that he was gone for good, I felt relieved that these interrogations would be postponed indefinitely. I hadn't yet begun to miss him when the next weekend he picked me up and told me that we would spend every Sunday afternoon together. When he was through with his list of questions, we'd ride in silence through the countryside outside of Baltimore, each of us, I was certain, trying to think of some way to begin talking again.

But my mother working, this was completely new. Although I didn't understand the financial necessity for it, I did understand that it was nothing to take lightly. Before we'd leave for an estimate, I'd stand on a chair, checking Sophie's navy suit for lint while she turned in front of me, and then together we'd set out on our mission, which,

I learned quickly, was not simply to count rooms and give an estimate for moving costs, but to convince each customer why he needed WorldWide more than WorldWide needed him.

"We're not the cheapest. I'll be honest with you right off," Sophie would begin when she presented her estimate. "But as the expression goes, you get what you pay for."

I'd watch the customer as he read over the quote while Sophie talked, the initial shock at the amount, then the doubt turning to a different kind of shock as Sophie began to describe the hidden clauses in *other* companies' contracts, the inadequacy of the boxes they supplied, their histories of hiring unskilled labor, of damaging valued irreplaceable-at-any-cost possessions.

She had one basic speech that she gave to each kind of customer, making only small adjustments. According to Sophie there were only two kinds of customers: male and female. When the customer was male, Sophie took her loose-leaf binder filled with selected competitors' contracts and pointed out their tricky, ambiguous phrasing. She didn't bother to show her binder to the women: instead she assured them that she would be supervising the movers personally as they loaded up the truck.

Sophie told me my job was to tell her how she did as we drove home together after an estimate. But it soon became clear to me that Sophie didn't really want my opinion; what she wanted was to tell me how she did, to fret and dwell on parts of her presentation that hadn't gone well when she thought she hadn't been convincing and to gloat on the beauty of her presentation when she thought there was no doubt that the contract was hers. I didn't always agree with her conclusions, but I was happy enough just to be part of the generally winning team (we had a 70 percent sales average) that I didn't really mind being used this way, and I didn't begin arguing with Sophie until I entered junior high and my mother's job began to embarrass me.

I had discovered that other mothers, if they had to work at all, were secretaries, receptionists, or most noble yet, nurses. But after dinner and on Saturday mornings Sophie told me to grab my homework, pulled her hair back into a practical bun, put on her navy blazer with the words "WorldWide Movers" embroidered above the breast pocket, and set off with the vigor of a new military recruit, past my friends' houses, across the city and suburbs of Baltimore with her clipboard and maps, while I slumped down low in my seat next to her.

Today as we drive to Irving's house, she reads the map with the same unnecessary intensity that I remember, marking our route over it in pen through Jamie's tracing paper, which she tapes on to the edges of the map just the way she's always done.

"Here's where the road's about to branch out into a Y. Stay to the right," Sophie says.

"I know where we are, mother," I say. "This is the same route I drive to work five days a week."

"There's no need to snap at me, Megan. I was just trying to be helpful," she says.

In fact, even though I'm familiar with Irving's neighborhood, I usually pass by the side streets quickly on my way to and from the office. He lives on a short street that I have trouble finding, and I end up circling a nearby block twice before finally asking my mother to guide me in.

Irving's house is nearly identical to the others on his block—a sturdy, practical, post–World War II brick colonial with a sunroom added on as an afterthought. Good, I think, no surprises. We'll pick up the camp stove and on the way back home, I'll talk to Sophie.

But as soon as Irving answers the door, I know we're not going to get out of there so easily. Opened boxes with wads of crumpled newspapers sticking out of them are piled up on the floor behind him. Empty living-room bookshelves are covered with layers of dust. Irving, a man whose body looks ill at ease in the jeans and T-shirt he's wearing, as if the clothes belonged to a teenage son or to him in a previous decade, has newsprint stains across one cheekbone.

"Oh, I see you're moving," my mother says happily.

"Can I help you?" Irving says. "You're not the box people, are you?"

"We're here about the camp stove," I say. "My mother spoke with you on the phone?"

"Right, right. Come in. Sorry I confused you, but with everyone off doing who knows what, I lost track of who's supposed to be who."

Irving clears stacks of newspapers off of the couch and tells us to sit down while he goes to find the camp stove. But Sophie cannot sit still. Despite my whispered protests, she peers into boxes, shakes her head in disgust. When Irving finally comes back with the camp stove, I am rereading last Thursday's "Style" section.

"It still works real well," Irving says, handing me the stove, ignoring Sophie, who's still staring into boxes. "And the fuel tank's new like I told the man on the radio. But what with the kids in high school now, we don't do much camping anymore. Not that we don't travel. It's just that we usually stay at motels instead."

"Mother," I say, "come have a look. Is this what you had in mind?"

Sophie has her hands on her hips now as she walks over to us. "Young man, could I offer you a word of advice?" she says.

"Who, me?" Irving says.

"You're using far too much newspaper. Bunching it up every which way is not going to protect your valuables. What you want to aim for are smooth layers between items. Think of the newspaper as a sunscreen that protects your valuables from getting sunburned."

"What?"

"An *expensive* sunscreen. Then use just enough to filter out the ultraviolet rays."

"Mother," I say, "I thought we came here to buy a camp stove."

"Well, let me have a look at it then."

I hand my mother the camp stove, and she lifts up the lid and stares into it with a disapproving look on her face as if she were a mechanic staring into a badly neglected car engine. "The wire supports still look all right, I guess," she says. "Grates could use some cleaning. I'll give you ten for it."

"Lady, it's fifteen dollars like I said to the man on the radio."

"Twelve dollars."

"Twelve?" he says. "How about thirteen?"

"Twelve fifty," my mother says.

"Okay, it's yours."

As we're walking to the door, my mother says, "Just one more word of advice. Streamline your boxes. Those boxes you're using over there," she says, pointing to the corner of the room, "are too big for one person to move efficiently. They'll slow up the loading process, and I'm telling you a trade secret now, which I shouldn't be, but if you're paying them by the hour, the moving men love them because it takes two men or a dolly to get them out to the truck."

"Is that right?" Irving says, looking over at the boxes she's pointed to.

"The God's honest truth."

When we're in the car I tell Sophie she shouldn't have done that.

"It wasn't worth fifteen," she says. "I priced new ones at twenty-five."

"I mean you shouldn't have offered him advice. He didn't ask you for any, did he?"

"Oh, Megan, when are you going to learn to loosen up a little? You spend so much time wondering what's right and what's wrong that it amazes me that you ever get anything done at all. If you ask me, he should be grateful. I'm willing to bet that he's lying, that his wife and kids are long gone. Did you notice there wasn't any good china, just some mismatched everyday stuff? And all those history books. Definitely a man's possessions in those boxes. And what woman would allow her dishes to be packed up that way anyway? And I should know. I've seen plenty of people in transition. I used to get good money for my advice."

"Well you don't anymore," I say.

We drive the rest of the way home in silence, Sophie staring out the window instead of at her map. I think about apologizing, but I'm still too angry to say anything. What I'm thinking is, I'm thirty-four years old, I have a husband and a daughter and my own problems. I don't need this.

When we get back to the house my mother takes her camp stove out to the tent, and I put dinner in the oven. I'm drying lettuce between paper towels when Frank and Jamie come back from the game. "Who won?" I ask.

"Don't ask," Frank says, opening the refrigerator and taking out a beer.

"We ate popcorn," Jamie says, "but it wasn't the buttered kind like at the movies."

"It's better for you that way," I say.

"Yeah, but it doesn't taste good," she says.

Jamie goes into the living room and turns on the television, and Frank hugs me lightly from behind. When we first got married and bought this house, Frank said that we should make love in every room as a kind of christening for our first real house, but we never did. Even before Jamie was born we made love only in our bedroom with the door shut, and more quietly than when our bed backed up against a thin, shared apartment building wall. Soon we had Jamie, and neither one of us brought up what was happening between us. Instead we just poured all of our extra love into her. It had gone on this way so long that before Frank left I had figured we had both made a kind of silent agreement between us about living this way.

During the time Frank and I were apart, one night when Jamie was staying over a friend's house, I met a man at a bar who followed me back home. Because his car behaved erratically in cold weather, he left it running outside. "It's just as well. My husband's playing cards with some friends. He'll be back soon," I told him, almost believing it. We had sex here in the kitchen, and even though the windows were shut against the cold, and I couldn't hear his car running, I knew it was out there in the driveway and I couldn't relax. "Aren't you worried about someone stealing it?" I asked him. "Just try to take it easy," he told me. "I'm married, too."

Standing with Frank in the kitchen now, I feel self-conscious about this memory, and, as if by creating a physical distance I can stop Frank from reading my thoughts, I pull away from him slightly so I can still feel the tips of his fingers on my hips but can no longer feel his belt buckle touching the base of my spine.

Frank doesn't know about the man from the bar. We haven't talked much about those six months apart. I like to imagine Frank coming home at night to that efficiency he rented by the week and thinking about the mistake he was making, how much he missed Jamie and me; of him driving past the house on days that he didn't have Jamie and wishing he could walk back in and rewind everything to the day before he left. Once I called him at the number he gave me in case there were any emergencies with Jamie, but when he answered I thought I heard a woman's voice in the background, her voice caught in mid-sentence as he picked up the phone, and I hung up. Later that night Jamie and I rented a movie about a retarded boy and his brother, and we both cried at the ending. The woman he was seeing didn't have any part in the way I imagined Frank living.

Since he's been back, Frank and I are more careful around each other. I find myself putting on my nightgown before Frank comes up to bed, and we no longer brush our teeth standing next to each other in the morning. Last week he walked in while I was taking a bath, and he apologized for not knocking first and walked back out, shutting the door behind him. As he closed the door I felt my shoulders get bumpy with chills and slumped down farther into the tub. Frank says he knows it'll take time to get things right again, and he's willing to wait it out, but there's more to it than that. We're not newlywed-shy again, which wouldn't be so bad. Instead it's as if Frank and I have, without discussion, each reclaimed for our private selves all of the things we used to share.

*

Did you get a chance to talk to her?" he asks now, letting go of me.

"No," I say. "I'll do it tonight."

"You know I didn't mean anything by what I said this morning," he says. "Your mother's all right by me."

"I know," I say.

Frank goes upstairs to shower, and I turn on the radio while I finish making the salad. I flip around the dial until I find the station that my mother listens to. The truth is that after Frank left, I listened to this station for a while myself, mostly on the nights when Jamie had ballet or when Frank was with her and I was home alone, when the house seemed the most empty.

Once I even tried to call to talk to the psychotherapist who was doing a special on separation anxiety, but the number was busy for so long that by the time I finally got through, the car show was on instead. "Make, model and problem," the man screening the calls for the car show said to me. It was probably just as well. The more calls I listened to, the more I realized that separation anxiety didn't seem to be the right words for what I was going though. What I had, I decided, wasn't anxiety as much as it was straight-out pain.

When I find the station today, people are still calling in selling things: an exercycle, a 35-millimeter camera, an accordion. I recognize the announcer's voice as the same one that hosts the car show, and I don't know why but I feel reassured by this. I look up the station's number and push the redial button on the phone until I finally get through.

"Selling, buying or both?" a woman answers.

"Selling," I say.

"From where?"

"What?"

"Where are you calling from?"

"Oh. Silver Spring."

"Okay. I'm going to put you on hold. Have a description and price of each item ready. And remember, no cars, no pets, no guns, and no more than three items. And turn your radio down. You'll be able to hear the show on your phone until you're up."

While I'm waiting, I try to stretch the phone cord so I can see my mother's tent from the window, but the cord isn't long enough. I try to remember what it looks like. Two-person, I decide. Thirty dollars. When it's my turn, I suddenly realize my mother might still be listening to this station, and I get nervous and talk so softly that the host has to ask me to speak up. "A tent," I say. "I'm only asking thirty for it."

I lie and tell him my name is Martha instead of Megan, but when he asks for my phone number, I think about how lonely I feel waiting for my mother's flashlight to blink out at night, and I decide to give him the right number.

"Is that it for you today, Martha from Silver Spring?"

"No," I say. "A camp stove, too. Twelve fifty. Oh, they're both as good as new," I add. "Hardly been used at all."

I hang up quickly and look at the phone, expecting it to ring immediately. When it doesn't, I try to forget about it and finish fixing dinner.

During dinner I watch Sophie carefully to see if she knows what I'm up to, but she's busy telling Jamie the story about when she gave a moving estimate to a man who collected toy trains. "He had those tracks running through the whole house," she says. "Right down the banister, around the kitchen sink, you name it."

"That's a little hard to believe," Frank says.

"Not to the professional it isn't. You should see some of the things I've seen."

"Still," Frank says, "the kitchen sink."

"Megan remembers, don't you?" Sophie says, looking at me. "She was my good little helper when she wasn't much older than you," she says to Jamie now. "She remembers a lot. Don't you, Meg?"

I nod my head. Of course I remember the train man. He slapped my hand away when I reached out to touch the caboose that was winding its way through the laundry room. Did Sophie see him do this? I look at her but she has gone back to eating.

The phone finally rings, and I run upstairs to take it in the bedroom, explaining that it's a call I've been expecting from a friend at work. When I get back downstairs, everyone is eating in silence.

"I've almost got that thing figured out," my mother finally says. "Lend me a few eggs, and I'll try cooking breakfast on it tomorrow."

"What's that, Sophie?" Frank asks.

"The camp stove I bought today."

Frank nods his head and Jamie asks to be excused so she can go play.

When the doorbell rings, Frank looks at me and says, "Is that your friend?"

"Must be her," I say. "I'll only be a minute or two. She just wants to run something by me."

When I answer the door, I find a woman and a boy standing there.

"I'm Rita," the woman says, "from the phone. This is my Petie, the one the camping stuff is for."

I pull the door shut behind me and walk with them around to the backyard.

"Hey, Mom," Petie says when he sees the tent. "It's all set up and everything. Cool."

"I thought it was hardly used," Rita says.

"Just the past day or so," I say. "We're airing it out."

"I don't know," Rita says. "It looks a little small. Are you sure it's a two-person?"

"Come on, Mom," Petie says, "just have a look. You promised."

Petie unzips the tent and crawls inside while Rita and I stand outside waiting. I look back toward the house, hoping that Frank and my mother are finding something to talk about that keeps them at the dinner table.

"Hey," Petie says, sticking his head out of the flap. "The camp stove's in here, too. Come see, Mom."

"Why don't you bring it out, honey?"

While Petie is crawling out with the camp stove, I hear the back door to the house opening behind me. I turn around to see my mother walking across the yard, her hands on her hips. "What's going on out here?" she says.

Because the situation is getting far too complicated, I decide I'd better come clean. "Mother, this is Rita and Petie. They're interested in buying the tent and the stove."

"Well, I hope you told them they're not for sale."

"You can't camp out here anymore," I say. "It's making everyone uncomfortable. Why don't you let Petie buy the stuff and you can stay inside with us for the rest of your visit?"

"What are you up to?" my mother says.

"Nothing, Mother. I've been trying to tell you all day that you can't camp here anymore."

"She's been living in the tent?" Rita asks.

"Mom, there's all kinds of other neat stuff in there. A Citizens Band and everything," Petie says.

"That is not a Citizens Band, young man," Sophie says. "And who told you that you could poke around someone else's things without permission anyway?"

"Don't talk to my son that way," Rita says. "*She* let him into the tent. Yell at her if you want to yell at someone."

All three of them stare at me, and then Rita finally shakes her head and tells Petie that she'll buy him a tent and a cook stove somewhere else, maybe even brand new ones from the Army Navy.

"I'm sorry about the misunderstanding," I tell Rita.

"I have a mind to report you to the station," Rita says. "They'll bar you from calling in again."

"I'd understand if you did that," I say.

"Well you can be sure I'm going to consider it. I bet they have a list for people like you," Rita says, and then takes Petie's arm and walks him back out to their car.

Sophie and I stand in the yard, watching them drive away. "You could have just asked me," Sophie finally says, turning and walking back toward the house.

I catch up with her but don't say anything. This whole thing has gone so badly that I can't even remember what I expected the outcome to be when I phoned in Sophie's tent. I'm no longer completely sure, but I don't think I had bad intentions.

Sophie and I stand by the back door, and, because this seems to be the least I can do at this point, I let her lecture me. "You never could speak your mind directly, could you, Megan?" she says to me. "What do you think I would have said anyway if you asked me to move inside? Did you ever consider the fact that I was trying to stay out of your way, give you and Frank a chance to get reacquainted? If my tent makes you so uncomfortable, I'll stay inside for pity's sake. I've got to be heading back up tomorrow anyway."

I have never seen my mother look resigned in quite the way she does now, and I am startled that I have brought her down to this so easily. "You don't have to leave tomorrow," I say.

"Look, I should never have come in the first place. You and Frank need some time alone to sort things out. This was bad timing."

"No," I say. "That's not it at all. You've got it all wrong. I wanted you to stay inside. That's what I wanted."

"What's going on?" Frank says, opening the screen door. "Everything okay with your friend?"

"Fine," I say, walking back inside. "Mom's decided to sleep on the pull-out tonight."

"It's my last night," Sophie says. "Why not splurge?"

"Well, I'm glad," Frank says. "About tonight I mean. Tell you what, how about I make some margaritas to celebrate."

I go into the living room to tell Jamie that her grandmother's leaving tomorrow. "But since tonight's her last night, she's going to stay inside with us," I say.

Jamie's circling pictures in her "What's Wrong with This Picture?" book. She has a piece of hair stuck to the corner of her lip, but because I read somewhere that mothers fuss far more than is healthy with their little girls' appearances, I resist the urge to push Jamie's hair back behind her ear. She's too absorbed in finding upside-down lions and dogs standing upright on two legs to acknowledge me with more than a nod. Sometimes I worry that she will ask questions about the months her father saw her only on weekends and I won't know how to answer them. So far she has seemed to accept Frank's departure and return with the same nonchalance with which she now accepts her grandmother's leaving tomorrow, but I know that her secret life that shakes her awake in the middle of the night when she is dreaming will surface in her waking life sooner or later. I don't expect to get off easily. "You missed the hippos wearing sunglasses," I say, pointing them out to her.

That night after Jamie is tucked in bed, the three of us drink margaritas and watch boxing on television. Frank has finally finished the project he's been working on, an entertainment center for the living room. He set it up while I was bathing Jamie so he could surprise me. He's placed the television set on one of the higher shelves, and I have to strain the back of my neck to watch it. The other shelves are empty still, and, although I know I should appreciate the effort that Frank's gone to for me, instead I feel annoyed thinking about the unnecessary work it will take to rearrange books and decorations to fill them.

"Think of boxing as a ballet," Frank tells Sophie. "The punches are only part of it." Later we get drunk, and my mother and I degenerate and shout things like "get him" and "watch your face." My mother and I pick our favorites by trunk color. We call her boxer Mr. Blue and my boxer Mr. Red and act more drunk and dense than we are when Frank tries to explain to us the correct basis for picking a favorite.

My mother is falling asleep on the couch while Frank and I sit in chairs on either side of her, watching the final round. I walk upstairs to check on Jamie. I washed her hair tonight and when I lean over to kiss her, she smells sweet and slightly chemical. When it was just the two of us, I used to crawl in bed with her and tell her stories about a lion who could sing and play the piano. Since Frank has been back, I sit on the edge of her bed and read to her before she goes to sleep. Once I asked her if she wanted me to tell her a lion story again, but she said that she was too old for that now.

"Come here and sit with me," Frank says when I come back downstairs.

I feel the muscles in his thighs shift with my weight as I try to get comfortable in his lap. Frank smoothes down my shirt and pulls me back closer against him. When I turn to look at Sophie, she opens her eyes and feigns interest in the boxing match. "How's Mr. Blue making out?" she asks.

I feel Frank's body jerk slightly as he tries to fight off sleep. After his eyes are closed, I lean away from him, against the arm of the chair and study his profile. His hairline has begun to recede, yet since he's returned he's been combing his hair back, which emphasizes the fact that he is balding. As I stare at him it occurs to me where I've seen this look—downtown when Jamie and I were shopping. Frank has made the decision to become stylish without asking me what I thought first. I wonder if this was her idea.

I get up off of his lap and go into the bathroom. My mother's earrings are lined up in pairs, forming three rows in the lid of Jamie's shoebox, which sits on the rim of the sink. Jamie has given each row a theme this morning: the top row is hoops, the middle row is long strands, and the bottom row is everything else.

I push my hair behind my ears and hold up a set of brass, ladle-shaped earrings against my lobes. My face is long and pale like my father's and these earrings seem to elongate it even more. Sophie's blue enamel, button-shaped pair sets off my eyes in a way that surprises me. I think about taking these, slipping them into my shirt pocket and playing innocent when Sophie calls me next week looking for them, but I don't do this. Instead I choose two earrings at random. I walk back into the living room wearing a heavy gold hoop in one ear and a thin silver triangle in the other. I walk with my head tilted down to one side as if the gold hoop were influencing gravity.

Frank and my mother are both asleep when I get back to the living room, Frank in the armchair, his head leaning back, his mouth slightly open, my mother on the couch, softly snoring. But it doesn't matter. I stand in front of the television set with my head still tilted to one side anyway. "Hey, look at me," I say. "What's wrong with this picture?"

iloxi

When she left, I wanted her to take everything with her. I left the window open in case she needed to look back in. There are no screens, and I can see all that passes by—people, sometimes something beautiful, a girl with shiny hair. A cat sits on my window ledge and licks her paw.

We swam in a courtyard pool that's deeper than it is long. I licked the chlorine off of her until she was smoother than a pebble.

Today my roommate George wakes me up with a water pistol in my face. "Get a job," he says, "or clean the house."

I get dressed and go to Maxwells, and Felicia is already there, sitting at the end of the bar. She orders another beer and pays for mine. Her earrings are made of purple glass, and her fingers tap the counter as if every song on the jukebox is her favorite.

"You should have been a drummer," I tell her. "There's rhythm in those fingers."

Her voice is chalk, and I'm sorry I've started her talking. I nod and study my drink. With Felicia, there is no need to listen.

It's still morning when I leave Maxwells and walk to the apartment where Catherine lived when I met her. I'm studying the curtains hanging in the window. Cotton, muslin. I cannot reach them. When she left, she took my fingers. That's what I mean by everything.

Felicia yells at me. She has followed me and has her hands on her hips and her hair knotted on top of her head. "Come on," she says. "I've got my brother's car. Let's go to Mississippi."

The car sounds like it will leave parts all over Route 10. Felicia is talking, telling me that I have become strange, leaving without a word and looking paler than a flounder. We're going to Biloxi to lie on the beach.

"She's not worth it," Felicia says. "I never liked her."

Felicia is driving, and the scarf around her neck blowing out the car window reminds me of a scene I saw once in a movie—a girl laughing wildly, driving with the top down until her scarf gets caught under a car wheel, and her neck snaps. "I'm not even thinking about her," I say.

"She took your guitar and she can't even play. The girl's a bitch."

I fool with the radio dial until I get some sort of country, easy-listening station from Slidell. Barbara Mandrell, John Denver. In forty minutes, we are far from New Orleans.

The sky is cloudy when we get to Biloxi. We pull blankets and a thermos filled with vodka and orange juice out of the truck. I take off my shirt and lie on my back on the blanket. Felicia has some sort of leotard on under her dress. She rubs sunscreen on her shoulders and squints at the sky.

She is talking, and I am settling into the blanket. "She's not worth it," Felicia says. "She didn't even have the nerve to leave an address." Felicia lies down next to me on her stomach, her elbows supporting her. She drizzles dry sand on my forehead in the formation of seagull wings. "You are getting very sleepy," she says, and suddenly I am.

When I wake, it's starting to rain and Felicia is building a drip castle by the gulf. She walks over to me, shakes her salty hair on my face, and drags me to the water to praise her castle. The sky is so dark that I begin to think I might have slept for hours. There are waves in the gulf, and we are the only people left on the beach. By the time we get back to the car, it's pouring, and Felicia is laughing at nothing so loudly that I tell her that she's drunk, and I'll drive home.

"The windshield wipers," Felicia says from the passenger's seat. "They don't always work."

I start the car and she opens her window, reaches out, and moves the wiper with her hand. "Manual," she says. "This whole goddamn car is manual."

There is nothing to do but sit and wait for the rain to stop. My head itches from sand, and nothing is funny for so long that Felicia finally stops laughing.

"Hurricane season," I say to her. "You dragged me to goddamn Biloxi in hurricane season."

It's only a tropical storm, the radio announcer tells us. It doesn't have a name. Still, we are stranded in Biloxi with broken windshield wipers, and the only thing I can think about is getting back home and checking my mailbox. Today I will find yellow flowers tied together with guitar string. Tomorrow she will send a fingernail tip in a gold bag filled with chocolate coins. She will come back to me so slowly that when I wake up and find myself moving inside of her, it will be as simple as breathing.

Felicia is counting dollar bills and telling me that she has a plan. We'll stay overnight to escape the storm. When I don't argue, we leave the car and buy sodas and corn chips at the Junior Mart. "This," Felicia says, "I have to have," and puts down four dollars for a plastic key chain with a mermaid on it.

At the motel, Felicia tells the desk clerk that we want the honeymoon suite. "Doesn't anything make you laugh anymore?" she asks me in our room. She turns on the television, then goes into the bathroom and closes the door. In the shower she sings in her voice that is chalk, and I read the bottom of the TV screen, reports about the weather.

I consider calling George and telling him I have work and won't be home until tomorrow—some new club in Metairie, maybe a permanent position, guitar included and amp that could crack the plaster in walls.

Felicia comes out of the bathroom with a towel wrapped around her head like a turban, her breasts pushed together under another towel. "Don't worry," she says. "I left one for you."

She pulls pillows out from under the bedspread, leans back, and eats corn chips. "Isn't this better," she says, "than driving home in the rain?"

"You should have been a camp counselor," I tell her.

"What's wrong with what I do now?"

I try to remember what she does. Some new job selling T-shirts on Bourbon Street, I think. When I met her, she was working as a bartender at Maxwells, and I was playing three nights a week—R & B and some straight country. Catherine danced by herself close to the stage, slow moves as if she were at home with the blinds closed, as if her body were sliding down a well. I close my eyes and imagine Catherine dancing by the bed, without music, just her voice somewhere quiet and removed.

"She was just a flighty girl from L.A.," Felicia says. "When she left she did you a favor."

Felicia opens the motel room door, and the rain pours down.

"Still a tropical storm," I tell her. "It'll be over by morning."

"I'm bored," she says. "Let's go skinny dipping. Let's get hit by lightning. Let's do something."

Now I am laughing, and it's such a strange, low sound that Felicia walks over to me and covers my mouth with her hand. "Quiet," she says, "I'll show you what love is."

Perm

used to be more of an idealist. Hair used to slip through my fingers, and I could envision a design, a style that would command notice. I'd say, *Talk to me about that picture you're holding. Tell me what it is you like about it.* Maybe it would be the color when I thought it was the wave. Sometimes a customer would get to talking about how the bangs fell, and I'd see it was the forehead she was really after, a high, smooth forehead. I might say, *How about a little lift on top? That might work better for you.*

Even when I was an idealist, I never followed the fads. I just tried to give my customers what they wanted. Now I tell them point blank when they have the wrong idea for themselves. How are you going to live with a pageboy on a long, thin face is what I want to know.

A lot of them bring pictures. The magazine glossies I can handle, but the pictures of themselves when they were younger and prettier are harder territory. *You might have matured out of that look,* I say. *How about something a little different?*

Not everyone likes my style. I've had to move around. But finally here at Lots of Locks I may have found my niche, which is too bad because my boyfriend recently moved out, and if this job weren't going so well, I'd be seriously thinking about leaving town.

People talk to their hairdressers. This is nothing new. I hear all kinds of things, but their hair problems are always worse than anything else going on in their personal lives. One woman's kid gave her lice with eggs so sticky they clung on no matter how many chemicals she shampooed with. When she came to see me, I shaved the nape of her neck and told her to make like we did it for body if anyone said anything. Now she's suffering from a frizzy home perm. I cut an inch all around every six weeks, and we talk about the style we're going to try when it grows out. *Forget anything blunt,* I tell her. *You'd better think layers for a while.*

My own hair I wear straight to my shoulders because it's easier that way, and with all of the time I spend fussing over everyone else, I'd rather leave myself alone. Considering my lineage, my hair came out quite pale. Corn silk, my mother used to call it, smoothing it down for school with her wet comb. Goldilocks. Her own hair was coarse and dark like my father's. Broken strands looked like cracked enamel in the bathroom sink.

My ex-boyfriend used to masturbate looking at the hairstyle magazines I brought home when I was still studying. It's true. I caught him doing it once, sitting at the kitchen table, a picture of some vacant, blow-dried model flat out on the table in front of him.

If I left town I might go to the badlands or New Mexico or somewhere else I've never been. I wouldn't mind getting some job outside, maybe cutting down tree branches, something that didn't require so much detail work, so much patience and goodwill.

These days I work late. I sweep up my own spot carefully. The manager gave me a key. Sometimes I arch back into a deep sink and run streams of warm water down the back of my head. I give myself a shampoo, towel dry, and then I'm out of there.

Ricky's moved just down the block from me. When I walk home from the bus, I look up at his window. The shade's always closed.

Once I saw him and his new girlfriend drinking beer on the front stoop. *Fine*, I thought, *degenerate. You go your way and I'll go mine.*

Although what we had wasn't great, I've seen worse. At night he used to fill a bucket with warm water and rub down my aching feet. I've worked on ladies who flinched when you so much as touched them, as if nothing human had ever gotten that close.

The funny thing is that the very pretty and the very ugly don't care too much how you handle them, what you do. They want their hair short in the summer because it's cooler that way. *What do you think?* they might say. *Give me something practical.*

Ricky's new girlfriend isn't much. She treats herself like a Barbie doll though, goes in for the accents—rhinestone barrettes, a big tortoiseshell clip. When Ricky and I were still living together, she used to call and ask for him when I answered the phone. She has enough nerve for five people. *I can't talk now*, Ricky would tell her while I pretended to be busy putting away the dishes and not even caring enough to listen. *I told you*, he'd whisper, stretching the phone cord across the kitchen. *Honey, don't call me here.*

It's the third Wednesday in the month, which means I have an at-home appointment today, routine like clockwork. Mrs. Gilford lives just next door to me so I can't very well not show up. She's confined because of her partial paralysis. Usually she's just a roll-and-set. Once in a while she'll surprise you, though. She might ask for a little color, and I'll have to go back to the shop and get it. We set up right there in her living room.

Her husband, Simeon, who's retired, loves her so much it hurts me even to think about it. They've been married forty years. He's hung their marriage license on the living room wall as if it's a diploma. He sits on the couch and watches her while I work. *You're going to look so pretty, baby,* is what he always says.

Tonight he serves us both dinner before I get to work. Beef stroganoff in July because she likes it. He boils those little egg noodles and pours the beef slices and brown sauce over them. My stomach turns, but I eat anyway so I don't hurt Simeon's feelings. Simeon is the kind of man who says right away, *Call me Sim.*

Mrs. Gilford is not as friendly, but she's a nice lady. Her way is just different from his—old school, more formal. She calls my customers clients.

"Dear," she says to me tonight, "tell me about what has been going on with your clients this week."

I try to make it sound like a soap opera for her. I tell her my boss had mascara stains under his eyes on Monday morning. I tell her about how many self-inflicted peroxide jobs I've had to correct.

"And how is that poor woman with the orange-stained hair making out?" she asks me. "Have you made any progress yet?"

"We're working with cellophane treatments now," I tell her. "I won't get near her with chemicals after the way she was ruined."

Mrs. Gilford shakes her head and clicks her tongue. You can tell it really does break her heart what people go through, how many bad hairstylists there are in this world.

Before I get to work, I hook a towel around Mrs. Gilford's neck and spread another one over the blanket covering her legs. She's so ashamed of her useless legs, she even keeps them covered in summer.

"We'll just go with a trim and set tonight," she says.

Simeon takes his place on the couch to watch. I fill a bowl with water and slowly comb it through her hair. When her hair is wet enough, I start to trim.

Mrs. Gilford asks me more questions about my clients. She goes through the regulars. "Any new ones?" she says. "Anything unusual?"

I am not at my best tonight. I am hard-pressed for more gossip, for anything interesting to say. I look over at Simeon, who's looking a little concerned. They're used to me doing more talking. I keep trimming. I'm clipping away.

When the edge of my scissors touches up against Mrs. Gilford's peach-colored scalp, it's as if someone else is attached to them, someone spiteful and untrustworthy. Simeon gets up off the couch and walks over to us. He gently takes the scissors from my hand, his mouth open a little, like he wants to say something, but no words are coming out.

All hair is, is just dead cells, I am thinking. I read that someplace. I can't remember where. I unhook the towel from around Mrs. Gilford's neck and gather up my things.

Her husband's hand is on her shoulder when Mrs. Gilford reaches up to the back of her head, rubs two fingers over her new prickly almost-bald spot and lets out a brief *Oh*.

Really, what else is there to say?

Acknowledgments

The author wishes to make grateful acknowledgment to the editors of the following publications in which these stories first appeared, sometimes in slightly different forms: *Chiron Review* ("Fumes"); *Clare* ("Cheap Clown"); *The Cream City Review* ("Aghast"); *The Florida Review* ("Naked Lake," originally published as "Naked"); *Indiana Review* ("The Visit"); *Jacaranda* ("Mr. Herzinger"); *Mississippi Review* ("A Good Bet"); *Mississippi Review Web Edition* ("Speed-Walk"); *Music From a Farther Room* ("Honeymoon," originally published as "Motel Pool"); *New Virginia Review* ("You Can't Dance"); *Pearl* ("Two Parties"); *Phoebe, The George Mason Review* ("Biloxi"); *Water-Stone: Hamline Literary Review* ("Perm"); *West Branch* ("The Queen of Laundry").

I am grateful to have so many supportive friends. Special thanks to Sarah Michaelson, Gina Caruso, Teddi Chichester Bonca, Cornel Bonca, and Angelin Donohue, excellent listeners and readers, and to Jan Kraft, Ginger Mazzapica, Anne Poppaw, Marcie and David Moody, and Madelyn and Michael Callahan, all lifelong friends. I also want to thank the members of my writers' group for their honesty and the implicit deadlines they provided, my women's research group at California State University, Long Beach, for their companionship and encouragement, the faculty in the MFA program of the University of Maryland, and my chair at CSU, Eileen Klink, for her support. I am also grateful to Deborah Meade at University of Pittsburgh Press for providing such a keen eye for detail.

In addition, I want to thank my family for letting me stumble and for sticking around to help me back up: Joyce and Gary Lott, Morton and Barbara Ann Greenberg, Larry and Kim Greenberg, Elizabeth Greenberg and Robert Blecker, Sean Carter, and Florence Feinstein, storyteller extraordinaire.

Finally, I want to thank my children, Joel, Claire, and Noah, for keeping me awake, tuned into the moment, and perpetually on my toes, and my husband, Michael, without whom—no kidding—this book would not be possible.